The
Cat Who...
Reunion
Cookbook

The Cat Who ...
Reunion Cookbook

Julie Murphy
&
Sally Abney Stempinski

Berkley Prime Crime
New York

THE BERKLEY PUBLISHING GROUP
Published by the Penguin Group
Penguin Group (USA) Inc.
375 Hudson Street, New York, New York 10014, USA
Penguin Group (Canada), 90 Eglinton Avenue East, Suite 700, Toronto, Ontario M4P 2Y3, Canada
   (a division of Pearson Penguin Canada Inc.)
Penguin Books Ltd., 80 Strand, London WC2R 0RL, England
Penguin Group Ireland, 25 St. Stephen's Green, Dublin 2, Ireland (a division of Penguin Books Ltd.)
Penguin Group (Australia), 250 Camberwell Road, Camberwell, Victoria 3124, Australia (a division of Pearson Australia Group Pty. Ltd.)
Penguin Books India Pvt. Ltd., 11 Community Centre, Panchsheel Park, New Delhi—110 017, India
Penguin Group (NZ), Cnr. Airborne and Rosedale Roads, Albany, Auckland 1310, New Zealand (a division of Pearson New Zealand Ltd.)
Penguin Books (South Africa) (Pty.) Ltd., 24 Sturdee Avenue, Rosebank, Johannesburg 2196, South Africa

Penguin Books Ltd., Registered Offices: 80 Strand, London WC2R 0RL, England

This book is an original publication of The Berkley Publishing Group.

This is a work of fiction. Names, characters, places, and incidents either are the product of the author's imagination or are used fictitiously, and any resemblance to actual persons, living or dead, business establishments, events, or locales is entirely coincidental. The publisher does not have any control over and does not assume any responsibility for author or third-party websites or their content.

PUBLISHER'S NOTE: The recipes contained in this book are to be followed exactly as written. The publisher is not responsible for your specific health or allergy needs that may require medical supervision. The publisher is not responsible for any adverse reactions to the recipes contained in this book.

First edition: October 2006

Library of Congress Cataloging-in-Publication Data

Murphy, Julie.
    The cat who—went to a reunion cookbook / by Julie Murphy and Sally Abney Stempinski.
       p. cm.
ISBN 0-425-21188-6
1. Cookery. I. Stempinski, Sally Abney. II. Title.
TX714.M8683 2006
641.5—dc22   2006008997

PRINTED IN THE UNITED STATES OF AMERICA

10 9 8 7 6 5 4 3 2 1

A Special Note to the Reader

THERE'S A WEALTH of good food up there in Moose County, 400 miles north of everywhere. The recipes are buried in old family kitchens, gourmet restaurants, and the imagination of folks who read *The Cat Who . . .* books. Sally and Julie have staged a mining expedition.

If Mildred Riker, food editor of *The Moose County Something*, were here, she would cheer their accomplishment!

If Qwilleran were here, he'd write a "Qwill Pen" in praise of *The Cat Who . . . Reunion Cookbook.*

If Koko were here, he'd say, "YOW!"

—Lilian Jackson Braun

Dedication

WE CANNOT WRITE a family reunion cookbook without thinking about our own wonderful family and the many happy hours we have spent around the table talking, reminiscing, and sharing food. We have fond memories of family reunions and anticipate many more gatherings of our extended family and our dear family of friends.

Special thanks and love go to Olivia and Davis, who are a joy and a treasure. Love to Steve, Diane, Nickie, and Elyse for a lifetime shared. And love to Dale, Merry Carol, Jerry, Jan, Tina, Luanne, Troy, Merry Anne, Lori, Billy, Marlene, Shelley, Kathy, Lisa, Betty, Diane, Susan, and their families who know they always have a place in our hearts and at our tables for dinner.

This cookbook is dedicated with fond memories to Grandma Polen and her "spiked" punch, endless pots of potato soup, and her soft cookies in the cookie jar. It is also dedicated to Grandma Irene and her love of trying new foods and sharing them with family and friends. We will always remember her yard parties, Christmas and Thanksgiving dinners, fire-pit beans, and crème de menthe. We make her hasenpfeffer, pheasant in cream sauce, and mustard-battered fried fish, evoking wonderful Bandy Road memories. We remember Grandma Stempinski and her freezer full of delicious cabbage rolls. The simmering aroma of her specialty brings back memories of festive holiday family gatherings.

We also express our gratitude to our family of friends who have supported us with friendship, fellowship, and tasting. Thank you for your suggestions and for sharing stories from your own family reunions. Thanks to the cropping ladies, faculty and staff at Tyrone, Eating Cardinals, First Christian Church, ACC faculty, Jon, Bill, Nancy, and Dorothy.

A heartfelt thank-you goes to Lilian Jackson Braun for making us all feel like a part of her Moose County family. How wonderful it is to get to visit Moose County to catch up with all the news and happenings of Qwill and friends. We are all fortunate, indeed, to be a part of this literary family.

DEDICATION

Contents

Preface

Yes, there really is a place called Moose County, 400 miles north of everywhere. The county seat is Pickax City, population three thousand.

There really is a busboy named Derek Cuttlebrink. And there is a barkeeper who looks like a bear and charges a nickel for a paper napkin. And there is a cat named Kao K'o Kung, who is smarter than people.

If they sound like characters in a play, that's because . . . "All the world's a stage, and all the men and women merely players." (**Sniffed Glue**)

Mildred said, "I hear there'll be several family reunions during the summer, and I thought I might run a series of features on the food preferences of each group—with recipes." She looked at Qwilleran speculatively. "Would the K Fund be interested in publishing a cookbook?"

"Absolutely! And I'll volunteer as official taster." (**Dropped a Bombshell**)

"What is it that draws so many relatives together—from such great distances? [asked Quwill-eran] It must be an emotion I've never felt."

"I daresay. It all boils down to family feeling—a consuming interest in your own flesh and blood—their successes, exploits, travels, even setbacks—a chance to see how the kids have grown, who has dyed her hair, who is gaining weight." [answered Thornton Haggis] (**Dropped a Bombshell**)

[As Quwilleran says to Koko and Yum Yum], "How about a read?" (**Came to Breakfast**)

Acknowledgments

We would like to gratefully acknowledge our editor, Natalee Rosenstein, for her support of this endeavor.

Special acknowledgment goes to Jeannie and Abby for their encouragement.

And last, we acknowledge Jim, Scottie, and Amanda. You are appreciated.

Introduction

*R*EUNIONS GIVE US a welcome opportunity to get together with family and friends. We find out what's been happening since the last time we gathered. We laugh and cry and share our lives. And, we get to eat delicious foods as we share a meal. We may bring foods made from new recipes but can never forget the old family favorites.

We've selected the best-loved families of Moose County for a literary reunion. Reuniting with our friends from our favorite books can be just as delightful as getting together with real-life family and friends. As you read through *The Cat Who . . . Reunion Cookbook,* you can revisit some favorite moments with the characters while reading the quotes found in books from the beloved *Cat Who . . .* novels by Lilian Jackson Braun.

While revisiting the families, you can enjoy the flavor of their favorite foods. Try some Scottish shortbread with the Brodies. Have some potato salad with Celia and Mr. O'Dell. For an adventure, prepare the longest antipasto tray from Derek's long, tall family reunion. Be ready for some unexpected delights as Koko and Yum Yum prepare for a feline reunion.

Whether it's a literary reunion, a family reunion, or even a cat reunion, we hope you enjoy these specialties from our Moose County friends.

The
Cat Who ...
Reunion
Cookbook

Ogilvie–Fugtree Reunion

Mitch and Kristi invite you to a family reunion at the Fugtree farmhouse on July 20th at 1:00.

Be ready for badminton, horseshoes, softball, touch football, sack races, three-legged races, baby crawling races, checkers, cards, and much more.

The meats will be catered. Bring your favorite side dish or dessert.

"How many families have signed up, Thorn? [to hold a reunion] Could I spend a morning or afternoon with one group—just to see what they do, what they talk about, what they eat, how far they've traveled to be part of Pickax Now?" [asked Qwilleran]

"Take your pick!" said the registrar. "Anyone of them would think it an honor. Here's the list."

"Ogilvie–Fugtree" sounded inviting. He had known Mitch Ogilvie when the young bachelor was managing the Farmhouse Museum and later when he was married to a descendant of Captain Fugtree. She was a goat farmer, and Mitch was learning to make cheese. They lived in the captain's historic farmhouse—a tall, stately, Victorian mansion. . . . According to legend, a "maiden in distress" once flung herself from the tower "on a dark and stormy night."

"Sign me up for a Saturday afternoon visit, Thorn," he said.

When Qwilleran drove to the reunion on Saturday afternoon, he could hear sounds of revelry in the quiet countryside long before he came upon the scene. His first impression upon arrival was one of color, quite unlike the somber aspect of the farm in previous years, when Kristi's entire herd of goats was tragically wiped out. (**Dropped a Bombshell**)

Beverage and Bread

E-Z Tea

2 quarts boiling water
2 cups sugar
8 family-sized tea bags

Place boiling water, sugar, and tea bags in a bowl. Let steep for 15 minutes. Pour into 2 1-quart containers from which the frozen tea can be easily removed, such as a square or round plastic freezer container; freeze. When serving, remove 1 tea concentrate from its container and place in a gallon-sized pitcher. Add 3 quarts of water. Stir thoroughly until dissolved. Repeat with the other frozen tea to make 2 gallons. Recipe can be doubled or tripled for larger crowds.

The Victorian frame building was freshly painted in two tones of mustard, set off by a neat lawn and a split-rail fence. A bronze plaque gave the history of the farm, built by Captain Fugtree, a Civil War hero. New barns had been added, goats browsed in the pastures, and a new pickup truck stood in the side drive. (**Said Cheese**)

Hush Puppies

1 cup buttermilk
2 tablespoons cooking oil
2 eggs
2 cups cornmeal
1 cup flour
1 teaspoon baking powder
1 teaspoon baking soda
1 teaspoon seasoned salt
½ teaspoon salt
½ teaspoon pepper
1 teaspoon sugar
½ cup chopped onions
oil

Mix buttermilk, oil, and eggs together. Mix cornmeal, flour, baking powder, baking soda, seasoned salt, salt, pepper, and sugar in large bowl. Stir buttermilk mixture into dry ingredients. Add onion. Drop mixture by tablespoonfuls into hot oil (375 degrees). Fry until golden brown on both sides and cooked in center. Drain on paper towels. MAKES APPROXIMATELY 2 DOZEN.

Salads and Side Dishes

Cherry Cola Salad

1 15-ounce can pitted dark sweet bing cherries
1 3-ounce package dark cherry gelatin
1 tablespoon fresh lemon juice
1 cup cherry cola
¾ cup chopped pecans
1 3-ounce package cream cheese, room temperature
½ cup sour cream
¼ cup sugar
½ pint whipping cream
3 tablespoons powdered sugar

Drain cherries; reserve juice. Heat ¾ cup of the reserved cherry juice over medium heat to boiling point; add to gelatin. Stir until all gelatin is dissolved. Add lemon juice and cola. Chill until gelatin begins to thicken. Add pecans and cherries. Mix cream cheese, sour cream, and sugar. Swirl into gelatin. Chill until firm. Whip cream until soft peaks form. Add powdered sugar. Spread on salad. SERVES 6–8.

Now the grass was greener, the old brick redder, and the colorful attire of folks-on-holiday resembled a garden in motion. Dozens of celebrators were laughing, jabbering, running around, playing games, guzzling soft drinks. Men were pitching horseshoes, young people were playing badminton. Their elders huddled in lawn chairs . . . (**Dropped a Bombshell**)

Elizabeth's Fruit Mold

¼ cup cold water
¼ cup sugar
2 packages unflavored gelatin
1 cup boiling water
½ cup fresh lemon juice
1 cup sliced bananas
1 15-ounce can dark sweet pitted cherries, drained (or 1 cup fresh, pitted cherries)
1 11-ounce can mandarin oranges, drained
1 cup chopped pecans

Spray a 7×11-inch dish with cooking spray. Line with plastic wrap. Combine cold water and sugar in large bowl. Sprinkle gelatin over water mixture and let sit about 3 minutes. Add boiling water and stir; add lemon juice. Chill until partially set. Fold in bananas, cherries, oranges, and nuts. Pour in dish lined with plastic wrap. Chill completely. Invert on a plate to serve; remove plastic. SERVES 8.

Stoplight Salad

1 16-ounce package frozen whole kernel corn or 3⅓ cups fresh corn
1 large tomato, chopped
1 medium zucchini, diced
½ medium cucumber, diced
¼ cup finely chopped sweet onion
2 tablespoons mayonnaise
¼ cup sour cream
2 teaspoons cider vinegar
¼ teaspoon ground mustard

¼ teaspoon celery seed
¼ teaspoon salt

Place corn in saucepan and bring to a boil. Drain and plunge into ice water to cool. Drain and combine with tomato, zucchini, cucumber, and onion. Mix mayonnaise, sour cream, vinegar, mustard, celery seed, and salt. Fold into vegetable mixture. Chill before serving. SERVES 6.

Qwilleran thought it commendable that Mitch Ogilvie . . . paid attention to these oldsters, listening to their stories and encouraging them to talk. (**Talked to Ghosts**)

Sweet-and-Sour Coleslaw

6 cups finely shredded cabbage
2 tablespoons minced onion
2 tablespoons sugar
2 tablespoons white vinegar
1 cup sour cream
½ teaspoon salt
¼ teaspoon pepper

Mix cabbage and onion in bowl. In another bowl mix sugar, vinegar, sour cream, salt, and pepper until sugar is dissolved; stir into cabbage and onion. Chill before serving. SERVES 8.

Potato-Mac Salad

_____

1 cup elbow macaroni
5 medium potatoes
¾ cup frozen peas
1 tablespoon minced onion
½ cup finely diced carrots
¼ cup chopped celery
1 tablespoon dill pickle cubes
1¼ cup mayonnaise
½ teaspoon salt

Prepare macaroni according to package directions, drain. Pare potatoes and dice. Cook until tender, drain. Cook peas according to package directions. Place all ingredients in a large bowl and mix gently to distribute mayonnaise. Chill 3 hours. SERVES 8.

Mitch Ogilvie, looking bucolic in his rough beard . . . , came from a low sprawling barn to meet them. A few years before, he had been a fastidiously groomed and properly suited desk clerk at the Pickax Hotel. After that he was the casual but neat manager of the Farm Museum. Now he was the cheesemaker on a goat farm. (**Tailed a Thief**)

Vegetable Kebobs

_____

2 medium zucchini, cut into chunks
6 3-inch sections corn on the cob
12 whole button mushrooms
18 cherry tomatoes
6 onion wedges

1 green pepper, cut into chunks
2 tablespoons butter, melted
cumin and chili powder, or basil and tarragon

Place vegetables on 6 skewers alternating pieces of zucchini, corn, mushrooms, tomatoes, onion, and green pepper. Baste with butter and sprinkle with desired herb combination. Grill over low heat for about 10 minutes on each side. SERVES 6.

Corn Combo

1 medium tomato
2 cups tomato juice
1 tablespoon finely chopped onion
1 clove garlic, minced
1 teaspoon cider vinegar
1 teaspoon Worcestershire sauce
2 tablespoons brown sugar, firmly packed
¼ teaspoon chili powder
2 15¼-ounce cans whole kernel corn
1 15-ounce can black beans
½ teaspoon salt

Place tomato in boiling water a few seconds to loosen skin. Remove skin and dice tomato. Place tomato and tomato juice in medium-sized saucepan. Stir in remaining ingredients and simmer 15–20 minutes. SERVES 10–12.

Bean Battle Winner 1967
Anna's Best Baked Beans

————————

2 16-ounce cans navy beans, rinsed and drained
¼ cup molasses
2 tablespoons water
¼ cup ketchup
½ cup finely chopped onion
1 tablespoon prepared yellow mustard
⅓ cup brown sugar, firmly packed
½ teaspoon salt

Preheat oven to 350 degrees. In a large bowl, gently mix together all ingredients. Place in a casserole dish and bake for 50 minutes. Serves 6–8.

Bean Battle Winner 1975
Moonbeans

————————

2 large cloves garlic, minced
⅓ cup butter
⅓ cup all-purpose flour
1 teaspoon salt
1½ cups milk
3 15½-ounce cans great northern beans, drained, rinsed

Preheat oven to 350 degrees. Saute garlic in butter in small skillet. Stir in flour and salt; add milk, stirring until mixture begins to thicken. Remove from heat. Place beans in a baking dish. Gently fold sauce into beans. Bake 50 minutes. Serves 8–10.

Bean Battle Winner 1981
Grandma Lou's Secret Recipe Beans

4 16-ounce cans pinto beans, rinsed and drained
1 cup finely chopped onion
1 clove garlic, minced
1 tablespoon brown mustard
1 tablespoon prepared yellow mustard
⅔ cup brown sugar
1 cup ketchup
½ cup molasses
1 teaspoon salt
¼ teaspoon cinnamon
pinch ginger

Preheat oven to 350 degrees. Mix all ingredients together. Pour into bean pot or large baking dish. Bake for 60 minutes. SERVES 12.

Bean Battle Winner 1998
Mexican Beans

1 15-ounce can black beans
1 19-ounce can cannellini beans (white kidney beans)
1 clove garlic, minced
½ cup chopped onion
1 tablespoon olive oil
1 teaspoon chili powder
½ teaspoon dried oregano
½ teaspoon ground cumin
¼ teaspoon salt
⅛ teaspoon pepper
2 tablespoons tomato paste
1 cup chicken broth

Preheat oven to 350 degrees. Drain and rinse beans. Place in mixing bowl. Saute garlic and onion in olive oil. Add chili powder, oregano, cumin, salt, and pepper. Cook, stirring for 1 minute. Add tomato paste and chicken broth. Stir over low heat until thoroughly mixed. Pour over beans; mix well. Place mixture in baking dish. Bake 35 minutes. SERVES 6.

Bean Battle Winner 2006
Mitch's Barbeque Beans

¼ cup cider vinegar
⅔ cup ketchup
½ cup brown sugar, firmly packed
2 tablespoons brown mustard
1 tablespoon chili powder
½ cup chopped onion
⅔ cup beer or water
½ teaspoon salt
½ teaspoon pepper
2 15-ounce cans pinto beans, rinsed and drained
2 19-ounce cans cannellini beans (white kidney beans), rinsed and drained

Preheat oven to 325 degrees. Mix vinegar, ketchup, brown sugar, mustard, chili powder, chopped onion, beer, salt, and pepper. Put in saucepan and simmer for 10 minutes. Place beans in large baking dish. Pour sauce over and stir gently to coat evenly. Bake 50–60 minutes. SERVES 12.

Orzo Salad with Goat Cheese

1 cup uncooked orzo
¼ cup finely chopped onion
½ cup finely chopped cucumber
½ cup finely chopped zucchini
½ cup finely chopped yellow squash
1 cup halved cherry tomatoes
3 tablespoons chopped black olives
½ cup crumbled goat cheese
2 tablespoons olive oil
3 tablespoons fresh lemon juice
1 teaspoon dried basil
½ teaspoon tarragon
½ teaspoon salt
¼ teaspoon pepper

Cook orzo according to package directions; drain. Mix orzo, onion, cucumber, zucchini, squash, tomatoes, olives, and cheese in a large bowl. Whisk olive oil, lemon juice, basil, tarragon, salt, and pepper together. Pour over orzo mixture. Stir gently. SERVES 6–8.

Grilled Fruit

2 tablespoons lemon juice
2 tablespoons lime juice
4 tablespoons butter, melted
8 slices fresh pineapple
8 firm fresh peach halves
2 tablespoons brown sugar, firmly packed

Mix lemon and lime juices with butter. Place pineapple and peaches on the grill over low heat. Baste with butter mixture. Turn fruit once, basting each side. Add the brown sugar to the basting mixture. Baste once more with the sugar mixture a few minutes before removing from heat. SERVES 8.

Meats

Grilled Chicken Breasts

⅓ cup ketchup
⅓ cup soy sauce
½ cup brown sugar, firmly packed
1 tablespoon fresh lime juice
1 clove garlic, finely chopped
8 chicken breasts
oil

Mix ketchup, soy sauce, brown sugar, lime juice, and garlic. Stir until sugar is dissolved; set aside. Brush chicken with oil so it will remain moist while grilling. Place over medium coals. Grill 15–20 minutes; turning several times until chicken is almost cooked. Generously baste with sauce; turn and cook 5 minutes. Baste other side; turn and grill 5 additional minutes or until juices run clear. SERVES 6–8.

"Do you make an effort to entertain them?" [asked Qwilleran]
"As you probably know, Mitch is a good storyteller and I introduce everyone to the goats, who are really sweet and sociable. Also, Mitch explains cheese making. And then, you've probably noticed the games at the picnic tables: cards, Parcheesi, checkers, jigsaw puzzles —"
[said Kristi] **(Dropped a Bombshell)**

Barbequed Ribs

10 pounds pork spareribs
3 cups ketchup
3 cups water
2 tablespoons prepared yellow mustard
¼ cup finely chopped onion
3 small cloves garlic, finely chopped
3 tablespoons cider vinegar
¼ cup Worcestershire sauce
⅓ cup brown sugar, firmly packed
1½ teaspoons black pepper
1½ teaspoons chili powder
1 teaspoon salt to taste

Preheat oven to 350 degrees. Place in single layer in 1 or 2 large roasting pans. Bake 1½ to 2 hours. While ribs are baking, combine the rest of the ingredients in a saucepan. Simmer for 30 minutes. Pour sauce over ribs during last 20–30 minutes of baking. Double recipe for larger crowds. SERVES 6–8.

Sandwiches for 24

5 10¾-ounce cans tomato puree
5 cups water
⅓ cup apple cider vinegar
½ cup brown sugar, firmly packed
⅓ cup Worcestershire sauce
1 small onion, chopped
2 tablespoons oregano
2 teaspoons salt
1 teaspoon pepper
5 pounds lean ground beef
1 large onion, chopped
24 slices mozzarella cheese
24 sandwich buns

Stir the first 9 ingredients together in a stockpot and simmer for 30 minutes. While the sauce is simmering, cook the ground beef and onion together until the meat is no longer pink. Pour off the grease. Add the meat to the sauce. Simmer for an additional 30 minutes. Spoon onto bottoms of buns. Place cheese on top of meat. Place top of bun over cheese. MAKES 24 SANDWICHES.

Qwilleran asked Kristi how they handled overnight accommodations. She said, "The kids like the tents in the backyard, and the older folks sleep in the rooms upstairs. We've an elevator now. Others shack up with Ogilvie families around the county." (**Dropped a Bombshell**)

Hot Dogs with Chili

⅓ cup minced onion
3 tablespoons butter
3 pounds lean ground beef
6 small cloves garlic, minced
2 tablespoons paprika
3 tablespoons chili powder
1 tablespoon salt
1½ teaspoon black pepper
1 6-ounce can tomato paste
1½ cups water
hot dogs, grilled
buns

In medium saucepan saute onion in butter. Add ground beef to pan. Cook beef and drain excess fat. Add rest of ingredients except hot dogs and buns and cook 10 minutes over low heat, stirring frequently to create a fine texture. Spoon over hot dogs. SERVES 12-16.

Ed's Barbequed Pork

5-pound pork loin roast
garlic powder
salt
pepper

Preheat oven to 350 degrees. Rub meat with garlic powder, salt, and pepper. Bake until internal temperature of meat reaches 165 degrees, about 2½ hours. Let stand 20 minutes. Remove fat and dice meat. Serve with Moose County's Best Barbeque Sauce. SERVES 12.

Moose County's Best Barbeque Sauce

3 tablespoons finely chopped onion
1 tablespoon light olive oil
1 15¼-ounce can plums, pitted
1 12-ounce bottle chili sauce
¼ cup brown sugar, firmly packed
2 tablespoons fresh lemon juice
1 tablespoon Worcestershire sauce
1 cup seedless blackberry preserves
1 teaspoon paprika

Saute onion in olive oil. Add rest of the ingredients. Use a hand blender or food processor to blend ingredients. Simmer over low heat for 20–30 minutes. Serve with diced pork. MAKES 4 CUPS.

Brunswick Stew

4 pounds chicken breasts
2 pounds beef roast
2 pounds pork roast
2 28-ounce cans diced tomatoes, undrained
3 14¾-ounce cans cream-style corn
2 15 ¼-ounce cans lima beans, undrained
1 14-ounce bottle ketchup or 1 18-ounce bottle barbeque sauce
⅓ cup cider vinegar
6 medium onions, chopped
½ cup Worcestershire sauce
sugar to taste
salt and pepper to taste

Preheat oven to 350 degrees. Bake chicken breasts, covered, approximately 1 hour or until fork tender. Bake beef and pork roasts, covered, approximately 2–2½ hours or until fork tender. Cool; wrap in plastic wrap. Chill overnight. Remove fat. Chop the meats. Place in large stockpot. Add the remaining ingredients. Stir well. Bring to a boil. Reduce heat and simmer, stirring occasionally, until well done, 1–1½ hours. Serves 12–15.

The Fugtree name was famous in Moose County. The farmhouse had been built by a lumber baron in the nineteenth century, and it was a perfect example of Affluent Victorian—three stories high, with a tower and a wealth of architectural detail. The complex of barns, sheds, and coops indicated it had been a working farm for a country gentleman with plenty of money. (**Talked to Ghosts**)

Leo's Zesty Hamburgers

4 pounds ground beef
1 cup minced onion
2 teaspoons dried parsley
1 teaspoon garlic powder
1 teaspoon oregano
1 teaspoon chili powder
salt and pepper
16 hamburger buns

Mix seasonings into ground beef, adjusting herbs as desired. Shape into quarter-pound patties. Grill over low heat on gas or charcoal grill. Place in buns. Garnish with County Fair Tomato Relish (page 23). SERVES 16.

County Fair Tomato Relish

3 cups ground green tomatoes
½ cup seeded and ground green peppers
½ cup seeded and ground red peppers
1 cup onion, ground
4 teaspoons salt
2 teaspoons celery seed
2 teaspoons mustard seed
1 teaspoon allspice
1 teaspoon turmeric
1¼ cups sugar
1 cup apple cider vinegar

Mix tomatoes, peppers, onion, and salt. Let vegetable mixture stand 10 minutes. Rinse and drain. Place in saucepan; add spices, sugar, and vinegar. Bring to a boil. Boil for 3 minutes. Refrigerate. MAKES ABOUT 1 QUART. Use on Leo's Zesty Hamburgers (page 22) or other sandwiches.

Desserts

Kristi sighed ruefully. "My earlier ancestors made a lot of money in lumbering, and they built this house, but the captain was more interested in being a war hero, which doesn't pay the bills. When my parents inherited the house, they struggled to keep it up, and now that they're gone, I'm trying to make it go. People tell me I should sell the land to a developer for condominiums, like the ones in Indian Village, but it would be a crime to tear down this fabulous house." (**Talked to Ghosts**)

Kristi's Sugar-Top Brownies

1 cup butter
2 cups sugar
1 teaspoon vanilla extract
3 eggs
2 cups all-purpose flour
½ cup cocoa
1 cup chopped pecans
1 cup chocolate chips
sugar

Preheat oven to 350 degrees. Grease a 9×13-inch pan. Cream butter, sugar, and vanilla in mixing bowl. Beat in eggs. Add flour and cocoa. Stir in pecans and chocolate chips. Spread mixture in prepared pan. Bake for 25–30 minutes. Sprinkle with sugar. Cut into squares. SERVES 12.

. . . conversation turned to the art center's new manager—Barb Ogilvie, the art-knitter.
"A very good choice," Polly said. "She's well organized and has a pleasant personality."
(Smelled a Rat)

Barb's Cookies

1 cup shortening
1 cup brown sugar, firmly packed
1 cup sugar
2 eggs
2 tablespoons water
1 teaspoon vanilla extract
1½ cups all-purpose flour
1 teaspoon baking soda
1 teaspoon salt
3 cups quick-cooking rolled oats
1 12-ounce package chocolate chips
1 cup walnuts, chopped

Preheat oven to 375 degrees. Cream shortening and sugars, add eggs, and beat well. Stir in water and vanilla. Mix flour, baking soda, and salt. Add to sugar mixture. Add rolled oats, chocolate chips, and walnuts. Drop by heaping teaspoonfuls onto ungreased cookie sheet. Bake 10–12 minutes. Cool 2 minutes. Remove to wire rack. MAKES 4 DOZEN.

The manager of the art center had swiveled her eyes at him [Qwilleran]; Barb Ogilvie had a talent for using her eyeballs to get what she wanted. **(Went Up the Creek)**

Peanut Butter Pie

⅔ cup sugar
2½ tablespoons cornstarch
1 tablespoon all-purpose flour
½ teaspoon salt
3 cups milk
3 egg yolks, beaten
¼ cup creamy or crunchy peanut butter
1 tablespoon butter
1 9-inch commercially prepared pie shell, baked
½ pint whipping cream
3 tablespoons powdered sugar
½ teaspoon vanilla extract

𝕸𝖎𝖝 sugar, cornstarch, flour, and salt in medium saucepan. Stir in milk. Cook over medium heat until thick, stirring constantly. Remove from heat. Stir a small amount of hot mixture into egg yolks. Pour yolks back into hot mixture and cook 1 minute longer, stirring constantly. Add peanut butter and butter. Cool slightly; pour into pie shell. Chill several hours or overnight until set. Whip whipping cream until soft peaks form. Add sugar and vanilla. Swirl on chilled pie. SERVES 6.

First thing Monday morning, knowing that farmers rise with the sun, Qwilleran called Alice Ogilvie at the sheep ranch. He remembered her as the demure pioneer woman on the float, in a long dress with a wisp of white kerchief at the neckline and a modest white cap on severely drawn-back hair. (**Saw Stars**)

Pecan Squares

Crust
¼ cup butter
⅓ cup brown sugar, firmly packed
1 cup all-purpose flour
¼ teaspoon baking powder
¼ cup chopped pecans

Preheat oven to 350 degrees. Generously grease an 8×8-inch baking pan. Cream butter and brown sugar. In a separate bowl, mix flour and baking powder together. Stir into sugar mixture until mixture resembles coarse cornmeal. Add pecans. Press into bottom of prepared baking dish. Bake for 10 minutes. Remove from oven; set aside.

Filling
2 eggs, well beaten
¾ cup dark corn syrup
¼ cup brown sugar, firmly packed
2 tablespoons all-purpose flour
¾ cup chopped pecans

Lower oven heat to 325 degrees. Mix eggs, corn syrup, brown sugar, and flour together. Add pecans. Pour over partially baked crust. Bake 20–25 minutes or until center is firm. Cool in pan. MAKES 16 SQUARES.

Qwilleran and Big Mac pushed through the crowds to an open field where a sheep-herding demonstration was scheduled. A flock of a dozen sheep was being unloaded from a stake-truck belonging to the Ogilvie Ranch and herded into a temporary corral divided into a maze of miniature pastures. The shepherd was Buster Ogilvie himself, carrying a crooked staff. Qwilleran knew the whole family. The shepherd grew the wool; his wife spun it into yarn; their daughter knitted it into sweaters and socks. (**Dropped a Bombshell**)

Buster's Bars

½ cup butter, room temperature
¼ cup creamy peanut butter
1 cup brown sugar, firmly packed
1 cup sugar
3 eggs
1 teaspoon vanilla extract
2 cups all-purpose flour
2 teaspoons baking powder
3 tablespoons chocolate syrup

Preheat oven to 350 degrees. Beat butter and peanut butter in large mixing bowl. Add sugars; blend well. Add eggs, beating after each egg is added. Add vanilla. Mix flour and baking powder; add to sugar mixture. Spread half of the batter in greased 9×13-inch baking pan. Drizzle syrup over batter. Top with remaining batter. Bake 30–35 minutes. SERVES 12.

She [Barb Ogilvie] had long straight blond hair and the sultry eyes that Riker had mentioned. They were heavy with makeup, and she shifted them from side to side as she talked—half smiling when Qwilleran complimented her on the knit vest she was wearing. (**Saw Stars**)

Chocolate Pound Cake

1 cup butter
½ cup shortening
3 cups sugar
5 eggs
1 teaspoon vanilla extract
3 cups all-purpose flour
½ cup cocoa
1 teaspoon baking powder
½ teaspoon salt
1 cup half-and-half

*P*reheat oven to 325 degrees. In a mixing bowl, cream butter, shortening, and sugar. Add eggs one at a time, beating after each egg. Add vanilla and mix until smooth. In a separate bowl, mix together flour, cocoa, baking powder, and salt. Add dry ingredients to sugar mixture, alternating with half-and-half. Pour batter in a greased Bundt or tube pan. Bake 90 minutes. Cool 10 minutes before inverting cake onto cake plate. SERVES 12.

Fried Cherry Pies

Crust
3 cups all-purpose flour
1 teaspoon salt
¾ cup shortening
1 egg
¼ cup ice water

Combine flour and salt in a bowl. Using a pastry knife, cut shortening into flour mixture. Blend until mixture is coarse; stir in egg. Sprinkle ice water over flour mixture and mix with a fork until dough forms. Chill in refrigerator for 1 hour or overnight.

Filling
1 15¼-ounce can dark sweet pitted cherries in heavy syrup
¼ cup sugar
3 tablespoons all-purpose flour
1 tablespoon butter
oil
sugar

Drain cherries well; reserve syrup. Place syrup in a saucepan with sugar. Stir sugar and syrup over medium heat until sugar dissolves. Place flour in a small bowl. Slowly mix in ¼ cup of syrup mixture and stir until blended. Pour flour mixture into saucepan with remaining syrup. Stir over medium heat until syrup comes to a boil. Reduce heat; continue to stir until thickened. Add cherries and butter; cook only until cherries are heated through. Remove from heat and let cool slightly. To make fried pies, divide dough into 12 equal pieces. Roll each piece of dough into a 6-inch circle. Place 2 tablespoonfuls of filling in center of dough. Fold dough over filling forming a semicircle. Use water to seal edges of dough. Fry in hot oil until golden brown. Drain on paper towels; sprinkle with sugar. MAKES 12 PIES.

. . . "The Ogilvie clan goes back to the twelfth century," said Mitch with obvious pride. My family came here from Scotland in 1861." (**Talked to Ghosts**)

Inchpot Fourth of July Reunion Picnic

Red, White, and Blue and You, Too

What: The Inchpot Reunion
When: July 4, 2:00
Where: The Pickax City Park

Bring your favorite red, white, or blue picnic food. Lois will provide the pies. Don't forget your best Tall Tale for the story competition after we eat. Surprise judge this year! Then enjoy an afternoon of softball, footraces, horseshoes, dominoes, and family news.

"The Inchpot name goes back a long way in the farming community. The farm museum in West Middle Hummock has quite a few things from early Inchpot homesteads." [said Qwilleran] (**Went into the Closet**)

Beverage and Bread

Patriotic Punch

7 cups cranberry juice cocktail
1 cup sugar
3 cups orange juice
⅓ cup lemon juice
8 6-inch bamboo skewers
½ pint fresh blueberries
8 cups ice

𝓗𝓮𝓪𝓽 and stir 1 cup cranberry juice and sugar in small saucepan until sugar is dissolved. Pour all juices together and chill. Soak skewers in water for 1 hour. Drain skewers and thread blueberries onto the skewers to make stirrers. Serve punch over ice with blueberry stirrers. SERVES 8.

Strawberry Bread

½ cup butter, softened
⅔ cup sugar
2 eggs
1 teaspoon vanilla extract
½ cup sour cream
½ cup strawberry jelly
1¾ cups all-purpose flour
½ teaspoon salt
½ teaspoon baking soda
½ teaspoon baking powder
¼ teaspoon cinnamon

Preheat oven to 350 degrees. Grease and flour a 9×6-inch loaf pan; set aside. Cream butter and sugar. Add eggs and mix just until blended. Stir in vanilla, sour cream, and jelly. Mix flour, salt, baking soda, baking powder, and cinnamon in a separate bowl. Add ⅓ of flour mixture at a time to sugar mixture. Pour into prepared loaf pan. Bake 45–50 minutes. Cool slightly and turn out onto serving plate. SERVES 8.

Lois Inchpot was a buxom, bossy, hard-working woman, whose lunchroom had been a shabby downtown landmark for years and years. Her customers regularly took up a collection when new equipment was needed for the kitchen. And when the dingy walls needed repainting, they volunteered their time and came in on the weekends. To be one of Lois's "family" was a mark of distinction, and although Qwilleran never soiled his hands, he bought the paint. (**Went Up the Creek***)*

Salads and Sides

Pickled Watermelon Rind

watermelon rind
2 quarts + 2 quarts water
⅓ cup salt
3 cups sugar
2 cups vinegar
2 cinnamon sticks, crushed
2 teaspoons whole cloves
1 teaspoon mustard seed
red food coloring

Cut away outer green skin and inner red flesh from watermelon rind; cut remaining rind into 1-inch chunks. Measure 8 cups. Place chunks in 2 quarts water and salt; refrigerate overnight. Drain watermelon and place in 2 quarts additional water in a large saucepan; boil for approximately 30 minutes. In separate saucepan, combine sugar, vinegar, cinnamon sticks, cloves, and mustard seed. Bring to a boil and then remove from heat; allow vinegar mixture to sit for 15 minutes; strain. Drain water from watermelon rind and add strained vinegar mixture. Bring to a boil; reduce heat and simmer for 1 hour or until syrup is thick and rind is clear. Add several drops red food coloring for last 15 minutes of cooking. MAKES 1 QUART.

"That boy of mine!" she [Lois] said proudly. "Nothing stops him! He has mornin' classes at the college, and then he's found himself a swell part-time job, managin' the clubhouse at Indian Village. He gave you as a reference, Mr. Q. Hope you don't mind."

"He's going to be a workaholic like his mother." [said Qwilleran] (**Tailed a Thief**)

Red-Hot Gelatin

2 3-ounce packages lemon gelatin
½ cup Red Hots (cinnamon candies)
2 cups boiling water
2 cups applesauce
2 3-ounce packages cream cheese, softened
2 tablespoons mayonnaise
⅓ cup half-and-half

*D*issolve gelatin and candies in boiling water. Stir in applesauce. Chill until partially set. Mix cream cheese, mayonnaise, and half-and-half. Swirl cream cheese mixture into gelatin. Chill until firm. SERVES 8–10.

Behind it [the reception desk] stood four young persons in black blazers with the Mackintosh crest. One of them was Lenny Inchpot, who had been on the desk when the bomb went off and a chandelier fell in the lobby. He still had a slight scar on his forehead. Now he was captain of the desk clerks, who worked in four six-hour shifts. He himself worked evenings. All were MCCC students. (**Robbed a Bank**)

Red, White, and Blue Salad

1 3-ounce package strawberry gelatin
2 tablespoons cold water
1 envelope unflavored gelatin
1 cup hot water
¼ cup sugar
1 3-ounce package cream cheese, softened
½ cup cold water
¾ cup sliced fresh strawberries
¾ cup fresh blueberries

Prepare gelatin according to package directions. Pour into 7×11-inch dish. Chill until gelatin begins to thicken. In separate bowl, sprinkle 2 tablespoons cold water over unflavored gelatin. Let stand 3 minutes. Stir in hot water and sugar; stir until gelatin is dissolved. With mixer, beat cream cheese into gelatin; add cold water. Chill until partially set. After strawberry gelatin is almost set, gently add a layer of the unflavored gelatin mixture. Place strawberries and blueberries over top. Chill until completely set. SERVES 6.

Lois herself was waiting on tables, and when she brought his [Qwilleran's] order, he thought the pancakes looked unusual. He tasted them cautiously.

"Lois," he called out, "what's wrong with these pancakes?"

She stared briefly at the plate before snatching it away. "You got Mrs. Toodle's oat-bran pancakes!" She took the plate to another table and returned with the right one. "Do these look better? She put margarine and honey on 'em, but she hadn't started to eat." That's the way it was in that restaurant—informal. (**Went into the Closet**)

Nanna's Strawberry Salad

2½ cups hot water
1 6-ounce package strawberry gelatin
1 8-ounce can crushed pineapple, drained with juice reserved
2 3-ounce packages cream cheese
½ cup finely chopped pecans
2 10-ounce packages frozen strawberries, thawed

Stir hot water into gelatin. Continue to stir until gelatin is completely dissolved. Add juice from pineapple. Place in refrigerator until gelatin begins to thicken. While mixture is thickening, make rounded teaspoonful-sized balls of cream cheese. Roll balls in pecans. When gelatin mixture is slightly thickened, stir in crushed pineapple, strawberries, and cream cheese balls. Return to refrigerator until completely set. SERVES 6.

Shoe Peg Corn Salad

¼ cup vegetable oil
¾ cup apple cider vinegar
½ teaspoon salt
¼ teaspoon pepper
¾ cup sugar
1 7-ounce can shoe peg corn, drained
1 8½-ounce can baby green peas, drained
1 8-ounce can French style green beans, drained
1 cup chopped onion
1 cup chopped celery
½ cup chopped green pepper

Bring the oil, vinegar, salt, pepper, and sugar to a boil. Set aside to cool. Gently mix the rest of the ingredients together. Pour the cooled liquid over the vegetables. Refrigerate overnight or until cold. SERVES 6.

"Where's Lenny?" [asked Qwilleran]

Her [Lois's] voice softened. "He has classes 'most all day on Wednesday, and I don't allow nothin' to interfere with that boy's education. He'll finish school if I hafta scrub floors! Did you know he's workin' part-time at the hotel?—I mean, the inn? Six to midnight. And he's captain of the desk clerks," she said proudly.

"Someday he'll be chief innkeeper," Qwilleran predicted, knowing that was what she wanted to hear. (**Robbed a Bank**)

Macaroni Salad

2 cups elbow macaroni
1½ cups mayonnaise
1 teaspoon prepared yellow mustard
½ cup diced cucumber
¼ cup finely chopped onion
½ cup finely diced celery
2 tomatoes, peeled, chopped
3 hardboiled eggs, chopped
salt and pepper to taste

Prepare macaroni according to package directions, drain. Mix mayonnaise, mustard, cucumber, onion, celery, and tomatoes together. Gently fold in eggs. Add macaroni, salt, and pepper. Refrigerate at least 4 hours before serving. SERVES 6–8.

Hart's Cole Slaw

½ medium onion, coarsely chopped
¼ cup white vinegar
1 teaspoon salt
½ teaspoon pepper
1 teaspoon celery seed
⅔ cup sugar
2 teaspoons prepared yellow mustard
1 cup oil
2 10-ounce bags fine shredded cabbage or 12 cups shredded cabbage

Blend onion and vinegar on lowest speed in blender until finely chopped. Add remaining ingredients, with the exception of the cabbage, and blend 30 seconds on medium speed. Pour over cabbage right before serving and mix well. SERVES 8–10.

"Where's your busboy, Lois?"

Her son, Lenny, usually helped her prepare for dinner.

"Job hunting! He finished two years at MCCC and he'd really like to go to one of them universities Down Below, but they're too expensive. So he's job hunting."

Qwilleran said, "Tell Lenny to apply to the K Fund for a scholarship. I'll vouch for him!"
(Brought Down the House)

Cucumber-Radish Salad

1½ teaspoons + ½ teaspoon salt
2 cups cold water
2 cups thinly sliced, peeled cucumber
4 teaspoons prepared horseradish
1 teaspoon sugar
1 cup sour cream
½ cup thinly sliced radishes
2 tablespoons sliced green onions

Dissolve 1½ teaspoons salt in water in a large bowl. Add cucumbers and let stand 10 minutes. Remove cucumbers with slotted spoon and place in bowl of unsalted cold water to rinse. Drain cucumbers and place on paper towel; pat dry. Mix horseradish, sugar, sour cream, and remaining ½ teaspoon salt. Mix with cucumbers; add radishes and onions. SERVES 4–6.

When the drinks were served, Arch proposed a toast to Lenny Inchpot, who had won "the last bike race before snow flies." (**Smelled a Rat**)

Potato Salad

8 cups diced raw potatoes
1 teaspoon salt
1 cup mayonnaise
2 tablespoons prepared yellow mustard
¼ cup finely chopped onion
¼ cup prepared, chopped, drained pimientos
1 cup sweet pickle relish
½ cup finely chopped celery
2 hardboiled eggs, chopped

Place potatoes in large saucepan. Cover with water; add salt. Cook until tender; drain. Mix mayonnaise, mustard, onion, pimientos, relish, celery, and eggs together. Pour over potatoes. Stir gently to evenly coat potatoes. Chill. SERVES 8–10.

. . . "You know, Mr. Q, sometimes I think I'm jinxed. I try hard, but something always happens. First the hotel gets bombed by some psycho, and I lose the only girl I was ever serious about. Also, my job is bombed out for a year. The interim job you got for me turned sour when I was framed. . . . See what I mean?"

. . . "don't let me hear any defeatist talk from you! Nothing can get you down, Lenny. You're like Lois!" (**Robbed a Bank**)

Three-Bean Salad

1 8-ounce can cut green beans, drained
1 8-ounce can cut yellow wax beans, drained
1 15½-ounce can kidney beans, drained and rinsed
½ cup chopped green pepper
½ cup chopped onion
¼ cup sliced almonds
½ cup sugar
½ cup cider vinegar
½ cup vegetable oil
1 teaspoon salt
½ teaspoon pepper

𝕸𝖎𝖝 beans, green pepper, onion, and almonds in a 1½-quart bowl. Bring the sugar, vinegar, and oil to a boil in a small saucepan. Cool and pour over bean mixture. Stir gently while adding salt and pepper. Chill before serving. SERVES 4–6.

He, himself, having a journalist's compulsion to be in the middle of the excitement, went early to breakfast at Lois's Luncheonette. The place was crowded. Two cooks were whirling around the kitchen, and Lois herself was taking orders, serving the ham and eggs, pouring coffee, and making change at the cash register. (**Sang for the Birds**)

Apple Relish

2 red apples
2 green apples
1 medium onion, chopped
¼ cup apple cider vinegar
⅓ cup sugar
⅓ cup raisins
½ teaspoon cinnamon

Wash and core apples. Place unpeeled apples in food processor or grinder; coarsely grind. Add onion, vinegar, sugar, raisins, and cinnamon. Bring to a boil over medium heat; boil 7 minutes. MAKES APPROXIMATELY 2 CUPS.

Beet Salad

2 15-ounce cans sliced beets, drained, juice reserved
3 cups sliced potatoes, cooked
3 cups sliced carrots, cooked
1 small onion, finely chopped
½ cup sugar
2 tablespoons flour
1 cup water
6 egg yolks, beaten slightly
1 cup vinegar

Gently combine beets, potatoes, carrots, and onion. Set aside. Mix sugar and flour together in saucepan. Add water slowly while stirring; add egg yolks; mix well. Stir in vinegar. Cook over low heat, stirring constantly until thickened. Sauce should be smooth but could contain pieces of egg white. Strain, if necessary. Pour over vegetables. Toss. Chill and serve. SERVES 12. Use reserved juice for Firecracker Deviled Eggs.

Firecracker Deviled Eggs

6 eggs, hardboiled
juice from 2 15-ounce cans of beets
⅓ cup mayonnaise
1 teaspoon prepared yellow mustard
2 tablespoons sour cream
2 teaspoons fresh minced parsley
½ teaspoon salt
few drops Tabasco sauce

Remove shells from hardboiled eggs. Place eggs in beet juice drained from beets for Beet Salad (page 48). If necessary, add enough water to juice to cover eggs. Let eggs remain in juice for at least 4 hours or overnight. Remove eggs from beet juice and pat dry; cut eggs in half. Remove yolks and blend with mayonnaise, mustard, sour cream, parsley, salt, and Tabasco sauce. Put yolk mixture back into (red) whites. SERVES 6.

"'Lois's Luncheonette will cater, with Lois herself joshing and bullying the media as she slices a turkey and a roast of beef and makes sandwiches on real bread. Her son, Lenny, will serve the apple pie and coffee . . .' Do you think we have a story, Qwill?" [asked Dwight Somers] **(Went Bananas)**

Meats

Qwilleran said, "The producers won't have trouble finding their extras. There are more Paul Bun-yans per acre in Moose County than in any other place I've known!" (**Went up the Creek**)

Paul Bunyan Burger

1 pound extra-lean ground beef
¼ cup chopped onion
¼ cup cracker crumbs
1 egg
¼ cup ketchup
1 teaspoon Worcestershire sauce
1 teaspoon salt
½ teaspoon pepper
4 slices Cheddar cheese
1 unsliced round loaf bread
sliced tomatoes
lettuce
mustard
ketchup
tomato relish

Preheat oven to 350 degrees. Mix together beef, onion, cracker crumbs, egg, ketchup, Worcestershire sauce, salt, and pepper. Place meat mixture in the middle of a 9×13-inch baking dish. Shape into a large, round, flat circle about 9 inches in diameter and ¾ inch thick, resembling a big hamburger patty. Bake for 30 minutes. Slice bread horizontally so it looks like a giant hamburger bun. Place meat, then cheese on bun. Add desired condiments. Cut into 6–8 wedges. SERVES 6 . . . OR 1 PAUL BUNYAN.

He [Qwilleran] left the police station with a light step, knowing he had contributed vital information to the investigation, and he treated himself to a good American breakfast of ham and eggs at Lois's Luncheonette, with a double order of her famous country fries. (**Wasn't There**)

Sloppy Joes

2 pounds lean ground beef
1 medium onion, chopped
½ teaspoon + ½ teaspoon salt
¼ teaspoon pepper
1 14-ounce bottle ketchup
2 teaspoons prepared yellow mustard
1 tablespoon vinegar
3 tablespoons sugar
½ cup water
12 hamburger buns

Cook ground beef, onion, ½ teaspoon salt, and pepper together in a large skillet. Pour off any grease. While meat is cooking, mix ketchup, mustard, vinegar, sugar, water, and ½ teaspoon salt together in a saucepan. Simmer for 5 minutes. Pour over cooked meat and simmer for 10–15 minutes. Serve hot in buns. SERVES 12.

Qwilleran stopped for lunch at Lois's Luncheonette. The Tuesday special was always turkey, and Lois always sent a few pieces of meat home to the Siamese. (**Talked Turkey**)

Evelyn's Crispy Chicken

1 fryer, cut into pieces
1 teaspoon poultry seasoning
2 cups buttermilk
1½ cups flour
1 teaspoon seasoned salt
shortening

*P*ut chicken in a large saucepan; add enough water to cover. Add poultry seasoning. Bring to a boil; reduce heat. Simmer 10 minutes. Remove chicken from water and place in a bowl; let cool for 15 minutes. Drain off any water that collects in bowl. Pour buttermilk over chicken and let soak for 10 minutes. Mix together flour and seasoned salt. Coat chicken with flour mixture. Heat shortening in skillet. Cook chicken, covered, until juices run clear, approximately 30 minutes. Remove lid and fry until each side is brown and crisp, 10 to 15 minutes. SERVES 6.

"I'm going to dinner at Lois's, and I may or may not bring you a treat. Today's special is meat loaf." [said Qwilleran] (**Went Bananas**)

Pimiento-Cheese Sandwiches

16 ounces grated Cheddar cheese
⅔ cup mayonnaise
1 4-ounce jar pimientos, drained
dash garlic powder
dash cayenne pepper or to taste
12 slices whole wheat bread
lettuce, optional
tomatoes, optional
bacon bits, optional

Using a mixer or food processor, combine cheese, mayonnaise, pimientos, garlic powder, and cayenne pepper or put in food processor. Pulse several times. Spread on 6 slices of bread. Add lettuce, tomato, and/or bacon bits if desired, and top with the other slices of bread. MAKES 6 SANDWICHES.

Ham Salad Sandwiches

4 cups finely chopped baked ham
1 cup mayonnaise
½ cup sweet pickle relish, undrained
2 teaspoons prepared yellow mustard
1 tablespoon brown sugar, firmly packed
8 sandwich buns

Place all ingredients except sandwich buns in bowl and mix thoroughly. Place ½ cup of salad on each bun. MAKES 8 SANDWICHES.

"Today's special," Lois announced as she slapped two soiled menu cards on the table. "Bean soup and ham sandwich."

"Give us a minute to decide," Qwilleran said, "but you can bring us coffee." (**Went into the Closet**)

Chicken Salad

4 cups diced cooked chicken breast
4 tablespoons celery, chopped
1 cup diced apple
1 cup mayonnaise
½ cup sour cream
lettuce

$\mathcal{P}$ut chicken, celery, apple, mayonnaise, and sour cream in a large bowl. Mix with a spoon until mayonnaise and sour cream are distributed evenly. Refrigerate several hours before serving. Serve on bed of lettuce. SERVES 4–6.

Desserts

The restaurant was empty when the two newsmen arrived.

"What'll you guys have?" Lois yelled through the kitchen pass-through. "The lunch specials are off! And we're low on soup!"

"Just coffee," Qwilleran called to her, "unless you have any apple pie left . . ."

"One piece, is all. Flip a coin."
Roger said, "You take it, Qwill. I'd just as soon have lemon." (**Sang for the Birds**)

Lemon Cream Pie

1 cup sugar
½ cup all-purpose flour
¼ teaspoon salt
2½ cups low-fat milk
4 egg yolks, slightly beaten
1 teaspoon lemon extract
1 tablespoon butter
1 baked pie crust
½ pint whipping cream
2 tablespoons powdered sugar
½ teaspoon vanilla

Place sugar, flour, and salt in saucepan, stir to mix. Slowly stir in milk; continue stirring mixture over medium heat until it comes to a boil. Remove 1 cup of the mixture and slowly stir into egg yolks, a little at a time. Return egg mixture to the saucepan and bring to a boil; stirring constantly. Remove from heat; stir in extract and butter. Pour filling into pie crust; chill. To serve, whip cream until stiff peaks form; add powdered sugar and vanilla. Smooth whipped cream over pie filling. SERVES 6.

His [Qwilleran's] next objective: A piece of apple pie at Lois's Luncheonette, a good source of local information and comfort food. The lunch crowd had left, and Lenny Inchpot was clearing tables. He helped his mother afternoons, attended morning classes at MCCC, and worked the registration disk at the Mackintosh Inn in the evening. (**Smelled a Rat**)

Apple Pie

7 cups peeled, cored, sliced apples
½ cup sugar
½ cup brown sugar, firmly packed
2 tablespoons all-purpose flour
½ cup chopped walnuts
1½ teaspoons ground cinnamon
¼ teaspoon ground nutmeg
¼ teaspoon ground cloves
double crust pie pastry, unbaked
2 tablespoons butter
water
sugar
cinnamon

Preheat oven to 375 degrees. Mix apples, sugars, flour, walnuts, and spices in large bowl. Place one pie pastry in deep-dish pie plate. Mound apple mixture into pastry; dot with butter. Place second pastry over mixture; crimp top and bottom edges of dough to seal. Sprinkle top pastry with water, sugar, and cinnamon. Cover edges of pie crust with aluminum foil strips. Place cookie sheet or sheet of foil under pie to catch drips, if necessary. Bake for 20 minutes; remove foil. Bake for additional 30 minutes. SERVES 6.

Cranberry Cream Pie

1 3-ounce package raspberry gelatin
1 cup hot water
1 8-ounce can jellied cranberry sauce
1 cup sour cream
1 9-inch baked pie crust
½ pint whipping cream
½ teaspoon vanilla extract
2 tablespoons powdered sugar

Mix gelatin and hot water. Stir until dissolved. Add cranberry sauce and sour cream to gelatin mixture. Blend thoroughly. Chill until slightly thickened. Pour into pie crust. Chill until firm. Whip cream, add vanilla and powdered sugar; dollop on pie. SERVES 6.

Peach Pie

Crust
2 cups all-purpose flour
1 teaspoon salt
½ teaspoon cinnamon
⅔ cup shortening
5–6 tablespoons ice water

Preheat oven to 375 degrees. Mix flour, salt, and cinnamon together. Cut shortening into flour mixture until mixture is crumbly. Add water a little at a time, mixing lightly with a fork until mixture holds together. Form into 2 balls. Roll on a floured surface into 2 circles about ¼ inch in thickness and large enough in diameter to fit a 9-inch pie pan.

Filling
3 tablespoons all-purpose flour
¾ cup sugar
4 cups peeled, sliced, fresh peaches
1 tablespoon fresh lemon juice
1 tablespoon butter
water
sugar

Mix flour and sugar together. Place peaches in separate bowl; fold sugar mixture into peaches. Add lemon juice. Place one pastry circle in 9-inch pie pan. Add peach filling. Dot with butter. Top with second pastry circle. Flute edges together. Cut vent slits in pastry. Sprinkle lightly with water and then sugar. Cover outer crust edges with a strip of foil to prevent too much browning. Place pie pan on cookie sheet to catch drips while baking. Bake for 25 minutes. Remove foil and bake 20 to 25 minutes or until crust is golden brown. Cool. SERVES 6.

Kolaches

4 cups all-purpose flour
2 tablespoons sugar
2 cups butter
1 pint vanilla bean ice cream, softened
strawberry jelly

Blend flour with sugar. Cut in butter until mixture resembles fine crumbs. Add ice cream and blend. Form into 2 balls. Chill overnight. Preheat oven to 350 degrees. Roll out to ¼-inch thickness on generously floured board. Dough will be very delicate and sticky. Cut into small rounds with 2-inch cookie cutter. Make slight indentations in centers and place ¼ teaspoon jelly in each. Place on ungreased cookie sheet. Bake 12–15 minutes. MAKES APPROXIMATELY 10 DOZEN.

Raspberry Squares

1 cup all-purpose flour
1 teaspoon baking powder
½ cup butter, softened
1 egg
1 tablespoon milk
½ cup seedless raspberry jelly

Preheat oven to 350 degrees. Mix flour and baking powder in a bowl. Mix in butter until crumbly. Add egg and milk. Mix well. Spread batter in 8-inch-square baking dish. Cover with jelly and then with topping.

Topping
½ cup sugar
½ cup brown sugar, firmly packed
1 egg
4 tablespoons butter, melted
1 cup frozen flaked coconut, thawed

Stir sugars and egg together. Add butter and coconut. Spread on top of jelly. Bake for 30 minutes. Cool, cut into squares. MAKES 16 SMALL SQUARES.

In the mid-afternoon Qwilleran walked downtown to Lois's Luncheonette for a slice of her famous apple pie. Lois Inchpot was a loud, bossy, good-hearted woman who had been feeding downtown shoppers and workers for decades—in a dingy backstreet lunchroom. The shabbier it became with the years, the more the customers cherished it; they felt comfortable there.
(Robbed a Bank)

Red Velvet Cake

1½ cups sugar
½ cup shortening
½ cup butter, room temperature
2 eggs
2½ cups all-purpose flour
2 tablespoons cocoa
1 teaspoon baking soda
1 teaspoon salt
1 cup buttermilk
1 ounce red food coloring
1 teaspoon vanilla

Preheat oven to 350 degrees. Cream sugar, shortening, and butter; beat in eggs. Mix flour, cocoa, baking soda, and salt in a separate bowl. Add to sugar mixture, alternating with buttermilk. Add food coloring and vanilla. Pour into 3 greased and floured 9-inch cake pans. Bake 30–35 minutes or until cake pulls from edges of pans and center springs back when lightly touched. Cool on wire racks and frost. SERVES 12–15.

Frosting

½ cup butter, room temperature
1 8-ounce package cream cheese, room temperature
1 1-pound box powdered sugar
1 teaspoon vanilla

Mix butter and cream cheese until well blended. Slowly stir in sugar and vanilla. Beat until fluffy. Spread between layers, on top, and sides of cooled cake.

Grandma Tacy's Tiny Cheesecakes

1½ cups chocolate graham cracker crumbs
½ cup + 1 cup sugar
½ cup melted butter
3 8-ounce packages cream cheese
3 eggs
1 teaspoon vanilla
15 strawberries
½ pint fresh blueberries
½ cup apple jelly

Preheat oven to 350 degrees. Mix together graham cracker crumbs, ½ cup sugar, and butter. Press 1 tablespoon of the crumb mixture into the bottoms and slightly up the sides in each of 30 muffin-tin cups. In mixing bowl, blend together cream cheese and 1 cup sugar. Mix in eggs and vanilla. Beat until smooth. Divide cheese mixture evenly among the cups. Bake cheesecakes for 20–22 minutes. Cool. Remove from pans and place on serving dish. Remove stems from strawberries and cut each in half. Place half strawberry and 3 blueberries on each cheesecake. Melt apple jelly in microwave oven. Drizzle about 1 teaspoonful over the fruit on each cheesecake. Chill 2 hours. MAKES 30.

. . . the mayor had recently proclaimed a Lois Inchpot Day in recognition of her thirty years of feeding hungry Pickaxians. (**Sang for the Birds**)

Brodie Family Reunion

Andy and Mattie invite you to the Brodie Family Reunion. We'll enjoy the first day of the Scottish Gathering and then have dinner together at the Scottish Hall at 7:00. Bring traditional Scottish food or your family favorite. It won't be the same unless you're there.

Be prepared for our annual version of our own Scottish games. Here are this year's events: mother-daughter lookalike contest, longest hair, longest beard, heaviest purse, fattest wallet, oldest family member, and other special events.

"... the tri-county Scottish Gathering and Highland Games would be held at the fairgrounds: bagpipes skirling, strong men in kilts tossing the caber, and pretty young women dancing the Highland Fling on the balls of their feet."

It was the first time Qwilleran had attended a Scottish Gathering and the first time one had been held in Moose County . . . There was more to the annual Scottish Gathering than competition, of course. It was a gathering of clans, a renewal of friendships, a scene of festivity. There were crowds of happy celebrators, Scottish food and drink, hospitality tents in bold colors, pennants flapping in the breeze, fiddlers fiddling, bagpipers piping. (**Robbed a Bank**)

Brodie was a popular lawman, an amiable Scot with a towering figure, a beefy chest, and sturdy legs that looked appropriate with the kilt, tam-o-shanter, and bagpipe that he brought out for parades and weddings.

Fran was tall like her father, with the same gray eyes and strawberry-blond hair, but her eyes had a steely glint of ambition and determination. (**Sniffed Glue**)

Beverage and Bread

Cran-Raspberry Tea

4 family-sized tea bags
2 cups boiling water
2 11½-ounce cans cranberry raspberry frozen concentrated juice, thawed
½ cup sugar
12 cups cold water

Add tea bags to boiling water. Let steep for 15 minutes. Remove tea bags and add more water, to make 2 cups. Mix tea, juice concentrate, sugar, and cold water in a gallon container. Chill. MAKES 1 GALLON.

Although the sheriff's deputies were courteous and cooperative, only the Pickax police chief [Andrew Brodie] could be depended upon for friendly conversation and off-the-record information. (**Sniffed Glue**)

Fran was the most glamorous woman in town, a talented member of the theater club, the police chief's daughter, and second in command at Amanda's Studio of Interior Design. (**Went Bananas**)

Cheese Scones

2 cups all-purpose flour
1 tablespoon baking powder
½ teaspoon dry mustard
¼ teaspoon cayenne pepper
½ teaspoon salt
3 tablespoons butter
1 egg, beaten
3 tablespoons cream
¼ cup sour cream
1 cup grated Cheddar cheese

Preheat oven to 400 degrees. In a large bowl mix together flour, baking powder, dry mustard, cayenne pepper, and salt. Add butter and blend until crumbly. Whisk together egg, cream, and sour cream in a separate bowl. Mix thoroughly with dry ingredients until dough forms. Add cheese and blend well. Place on a floured surface and pat into an 8-inch round. Transfer dough to greased cookie sheet. Cut into 8 wedges and pull wedges out slightly on cookie sheet so that edges are not touching. Bake 15 minutes. SERVES 8.

"Take my three girls, for instance. The two older ones got married right after school and start-ed families. I've got four grandkids, and I'm not fifty yet. But Francesca! She was the third. She was determined to go away to college and have a career." [said Brodie] (**Sniffed Glue**)

Then the talk turned to the inn: how it had been dreary but clean, how everyone hated the food, how Fran Brodie had worked wonders with the interior.
"She's one of our civic treasures," Qwilleran said.
"Yeah, she's a dynamo! Is she married?" [asked Barry]
"No, but they're standing in line. Take a number." (**Robbed a Bank**)

Salads and Side Dishes

Fran's Apricot Smoothie Gelatin

2 8¾-ounce cans apricots
water
2 3-ounce packages apricot gelatin
1 cup miniature marshmallows
lettuce

Drain apricots, reserving the juice; add water to make three cups. Heat the juice over medium heat until it comes to a boil. Place gelatin and marshmallows in a mixing bowl. Pour the hot juice over the gelatin and marshmallows; stir until dissolved. Chill until partially set. Puree the apricots with a hand blender or food processor; fold in gelatin mixture. Place gelatin in a 7×11-inch dish. Chill until completely set. To serve, cut into squares and serve on lettuce. SERVES 8.

"Bring your wife over some evening. She'll enjoy seeing Fran's work." [said Qwilleran]

"Did my daughter pick out all this furniture?" Brodie asked, more in dismay than admiration.

"She gets all the credit. She has a good eye and good taste." (**Knew a Cardinal**)

As Fran gave Qwilleran a theatrical goodnight kiss, he said to her, "Was this party your idea? Did you ring my phone a couple of times and hang up?"

"We had to be sure you were here, Qwill. We thought you might be out with Polly. Where is Polly tonight?"

"In Lockmaster at a wedding."

"Oh, really? Why didn't you go?" she asked slyly. "Afraid you'd catch the bouquet?" (**Knew a Cardinal**)

Blueberry-Lemon Salad

1 *3-ounce package lemon gelatin*
1 cup boiling water
½ cup whipping cream, whipped
½ cup cottage cheese
¼ cup pecans
1 cup blueberries

Stir gelatin and water until gelatin is completely dissolved; cool. Mix in the whipped cream and cottage cheese. Chill until partially set; add pecans and blueberries. Chill until completely set. SERVES 4–6.

Fran's strategy was all too transparent. She had asked for a key to his [Qwilleran's] apartment, in order, she said, to supervise the workmen and the delivery of merchandise. She brought wallpaper-sample books and furniture catalogues for his perusal, entailing consultations in close proximity on the sofa, with pictures and patterns spread out on their laps and with knees accidentally touching. She timed these tête-à-têtes for the cocktail hour, when it was only polite for Qwilleran to offer a drink or two, after which a dinner invitation was almost obligatory. (**Sniffed Glue**)

McIntosh Apple Salad

1 20-ounce can crushed pineapple, undrained
⅔ cup sugar
1 3-ounce package orange gelatin
1 8-ounce package cream cheese
1½ cups peeled, diced McIntosh apples
½ cup chopped walnuts
½ cup chopped celery
1 cup whipped topping

Combine pineapple and sugar in medium-sized saucepan. Boil for 2 minutes. Remove from heat. Add gelatin and cream cheese. Stir or whisk until both are dissolved. Cool; add apples, nuts, celery, and whipped topping. Pour into 9×9-inch baking dish. Chill and cut into squares. SERVES 9.

Cauliflower and Broccoli Salad

1 head cauliflower
1 head broccoli
1 large carrot
1½ cups grated mild Cheddar cheese
1 cup mayonnaise
1 cup sour cream
½ cup sugar
½ teaspoon salt
5 slices bacon, fried and crumbled

Cut cauliflower, broccoli, and carrot into bite-sized pieces. Place in large bowl. Add Cheddar cheese. Mix mayonnaise, sour cream, sugar, and salt. Stir into cauliflower mixture. Chill. Stir in bacon just before serving. SERVES 8–10.

Irene's Rutabaga

8 cups peeled, chopped rutabaga
2 tablespoons milk
4 tablespoons melted butter + 1 tablespoon butter
¼ cup chopped onion
2 teaspoons salt
¼ teaspoon ginger
¼ teaspoon nutmeg
¼ teaspoon dried dill weed

Place rutabaga in large pot of water. Cook until tender. Drain and mash with milk and 4 tablespoons melted butter. Saute onion in 1 tablespoon butter; stir onion and butter into rutabaga; add salt, ginger, nutmeg, and dill weed. SERVES 6–8.

Carrot-Rice Casserole

½ cup rice
½ cup orange juice
1 cup water
1 teaspoon salt
1½ cups shredded carrots
1½ cups shredded Cheddar cheese
2 eggs, beaten
2 tablespoons minced onion
½ cup milk

Preheat oven to 350 degrees. Cook rice in orange juice and water with salt for 25 minutes. Rice will not absorb all liquid. Remove from heat. Place carrots in greased 8x8-inch baking dish. Mix cheese, eggs, onion, milk, rice, and remaining liquid. Pour on top of carrots. Bake for 30–35 minutes. SERVES 6.

"Is everybody going to the Fryers Club play? [asked Mildred] It may be Fran Brodie's last production. I hear she's had a good job offer in Chicago." (**Saw Stars**)

Old World Kidney Beans and Kale

1 pound kale, chopped
2 15½-ounce cans light red kidney beans drained, rinsed
2 tablespoons lemon juice
1 teaspoon salt
½ teaspoon pepper
3–4 cloves garlic
2 tablespoons butter

Cook kale in large stockpot until tender. Drain and set aside. Mash beans just until they hold together. Add lemon juice, salt, and pepper. Sauté garlic in butter until tender; stir butter and garlic into beans. Add kale and mix well. SERVES 8.

Basil-Bean Salad

3 cups fresh green beans, cut into bite-sized pieces
½ cup grated carrots
½ cup chopped cabbage
2 stalks celery, finely chopped
½ cup finely chopped onion
3 tablespoons fresh chopped parsley
4 tablespoons mayonnaise
2 tablespoons fresh lemon juice
1 teaspoon dried or 3 teaspoons fresh chopped basil
salt and pepper

Mix beans, carrots, cabbage, celery, onion, and parsley. In separate bowl, combine mayonnaise, lemon juice, and basil. Stir into vegetables. Add salt and pepper to taste and mix well. Use additional parsley for garnish, if desired. SERVES 6–8.

"Actors get hungry. You should know that, Andy. You've been feeding one." [said Qwilleran]

"Not anymore," said Brodie with a frown. "Fran's moved out. Wanted her own place. Don't know why. She had it comfortable at home." He looked troubled—a north-country father who thought daughters should either marry and settle down or live at home with the folks. (**Knew a Cardinal**)

Skirlie Tomatoes

6 medium-sized ripe tomatoes
2 cups finely chopped onions
1 clove garlic, minced
⅔ cup butter
2 cups rolled oats
2 tablespoons chopped fresh parsley
salt and pepper to taste

Cut the top from tomatoes, scoop out and discard pulp; invert on paper towel to drain. Sauté onions and garlic in butter until tender. Add oats and parsley to onion mixture. Stir over low heat until butter is completely absorbed. Add salt and pepper. Place rolled-oats mixture in tomatoes. Can be served hot or cold. If hot tomatoes are desired, bake at 350 degrees for 25 minutes or until filling is heated through. SERVES 4–6.

Zucchini Sweet-and-Sour Relish

3 cups finely chopped zucchini
1½ cups finely chopped onion
3 tablespoons salt
2¼ cups sugar
2½ cups cider vinegar
1½ teaspoons ground mustard

Combine zucchini, onion, and salt. Cover with cold water. Let stand 90 minutes. Drain, rinse, and drain again. Mix sugar, vinegar, and mustard. Bring to a boil, stirring until sugar dissolves. Add zucchini and onions. Bring to a boil again, reduce heat, and simmer for 15 minutes; chill. MAKES APPROXIMATELY 4 CUPS.

"My old grandmother in Scotland could tail a thief with scissors, a piece of string, and a witch's chant. Too bad she died before I got into law enforcement." [said Brodie] (**Tailed a Thief**)

"I have confidence in Brodie. He grew up here, and he's a walking file on everyone in the county." [said Quilleran] (**Knew a Cardinal**)

Meats

Granny Brodie's Leeks and Ham

8 leeks
½ teaspoon salt
3 tablespoons butter
3 tablespoons all-purpose flour
1¼ cups milk
2 teaspoons brown mustard
¾ cup + ¼ cup grated Irish Cheddar cheese
salt and pepper
8 thin slices ham

Preheat oven to 350 degrees. Wash leeks and cut 1 inch above the white area. Discard green tops. Place leeks and salt into about 1 quart water and boil 20 minutes. Melt butter in separate saucepan, stir in flour. Add milk and stir until sauce thickens. Add mustard, ¾ cup of the cheese, and salt and pepper to taste. Remove leeks from water and drain. Wrap leeks in ham slices. Place in baking dish. Pour sauce over top; sprinkle with last ¼ cup of cheese. Bake 20 minutes. SERVES 6–8.

Scotch Pies

Filling
1 pound ground lamb or beef
½ teaspoon salt
½ teaspoon pepper
pinch nutmeg

Preheat oven to 350 degrees. In skillet, brown meat with salt, pepper, and nutmeg. Remove meat from pan, drain off grease, and set aside to cool slightly.

Gravy
3 tablespoons butter
3 tablespoons all-purpose flour
1 14-ounce can beef broth
½ teaspoon salt

Melt butter in skillet. Stir in flour until mixture thickens. Add beef broth and bring to a boil over low heat, stirring constantly until it thickens. Add salt. Add half of gravy to meat. Reserve remaining gravy to serve with pies.

Pastry
1 teaspoon salt
4 cups all-purpose flour
¾ cup shortening
¾ cup water, gently boiling

In mixing bowl, add salt to flour. Place shortening in center of flour mixture. Add hot water and use fork to blend till smooth. Roll dough on floured surface. Cut 12 circles approximately 4½ inches in diameter, and 12 circles 2½ inches in diameter. Place the larger circle in cupcake tins and flute the edges of each above the rims of the cups. Divide filling among the 12 cups. Place the smaller dough circles on the meat, using water to seal the edges of the pies. There should be space left at the top of the pastry to hold gravy when serving. Bake for 40 minutes or until crust is golden brown. To serve, reheat remaining gravy and place 2 tablespoonfuls onto the tops of each pie. MAKES 12.

"I don't know why you and Polly don't get hitched. [said Brodie] It's the only way to live, to my way of thinking."
"That's because you're a dedicated family man." [said Qwilleran] (**Wasn't There**)

"Another thing: we have good family life up here. We have a lot of church activities and organized sports and healthy outdoor hobbies like camping and hunting and fishing. It's a good place to bring up kids." [said Brodie] (**Sniffed Glue**)

Andy's Sausage Burgers

1 pound ground pork
1 pound lean ground beef
1½ cups fine, toasted bread crumbs
1 teaspoon nutmeg
1½ teaspoons coriander
1 teaspoon salt
½ teaspoon pepper
¾ cup water
oil
hard rolls

Mix all ingredients, except oil and hard rolls, thoroughly. Form meat into 2 rolls, 2 inches in diameter and about 10 inches long. Freeze slightly and cut into slices approximately ¾ inch thick. Fry in oil until brown. Serve in hard rolls. MAKES ABOUT 20 PATTIES.

When dinner was served, Big Mac leaned over and asked the chief, "Are you related to the master criminal of Edinburgh, Andy? I saw the place where he was hanged in 1788."

"Deacon Brodie? Well, I admit I've got his sense of humor and steel nerves, but he wasn't a piper." (**Wasn't There**)

"This year's parade will have flags, marching bands, floats, grass-roots participation, and a little originality." [said Mildred]

. . . "Who's the grand marshal?" [asked Lisa]

"Andrew Brodie, in Scottish regalia, with his bagpipe. He'll march just ahead of the color guard and play patriotic tunes in slow tempo." (**Saw Stars**)

Charlie's Scottish Fried Fish

2 cups oatmeal
1 teaspoon salt
½ teaspoon black pepper
3 egg whites
1 pound fresh fish filets
oil

Process oatmeal in a blender or food processor until finely chopped. Mix in salt and pepper; place oatmeal mixture on plate. Cut fish into serving-size pieces; dip fish into egg whites and then press into oats. Fry in hot oil in a skillet 7 minutes on each side or until fish flakes apart with fork. Serve with Parsley Butter.

Parsley Butter

¼ cup butter, softened
1 tablespoon fresh lemon juice
1 tablespoon chopped fresh parsley

Whip butter, lemon juice, and parsley together until well mixed. Serve with fish. SERVES 4. Can double or triple recipe as desired.

Lari's Honey Chicken

½ cup butter
4 skinless, boneless chicken breasts
salt and pepper to taste
4 tablespoons honey
3 tablespoons fresh lemon juice
3 sprigs fresh rosemary

Preheat oven to 350 degrees. Cut chicken breasts in half. Melt butter in skillet and brown chicken. Add salt and pepper. Place chicken pieces in casserole dish. Put honey, lemon juice, and rosemary into skillet that chicken was taken from. Stir and bring to a boil. Remove rosemary and pour honey mixture over chicken. Cover and bake 25 minutes or until done. SERVES 6–8.

Desserts

He [Qwilleran] found Andrew Brodie, the big, broad-shouldered chief of police, hunched over a computer, distrustfully poking the keys.

"Who invented these damn things?" Brodie growled. "More trouble than they're worth!"
(**Wasn't There**)

Scottish Cottage Pudding

1½ cup dry bread crumbs
½ teaspoon baking soda
½ teaspoon ground cinnamon
¼ teaspoon ground cloves
⅛ teaspoon ground ginger
¼ cup butter
½ cup sugar
½ cup strawberry jelly
2 eggs
½ cup buttermilk
clotted cream or whipped cream

Preheat oven to 350 degrees. Mix bread crumbs, baking soda, cinnamon, cloves, and ginger together. Set aside. Cream butter and sugar; add jelly and eggs. Mix well. Add bread crumb mixture to sugar mixture, alternating with the buttermilk. Pour into greased 8×8-inch baking dish. Bake for 40 minutes. Cool; serve with clotted cream or whipped cream. SERVES 8.

Tartan Cake

2 cups sugar
1¼ cups cooking oil
4 eggs
1 teaspoon vanilla extract
2 cups all-purpose flour
1½ teaspoons baking powder
1½ teaspoons baking soda
1 teaspoon salt
1½ teaspoons ground cinnamon
3 cups finely shredded carrots
1 cup chopped pecans

Preheat oven to 325 degrees. Cream sugar and oil together. Add eggs; beat well. Blend in vanilla. Mix flour, baking powder, baking soda, salt, and cinnamon together. Beat into sugar mixture. Fold in carrots and nuts. Pour into 9×13-inch greased baking pan. Bake 40 minutes. Frost with Cream Cheese Frosting (page 82) and decorate with plaid tartan. SERVES 12.

Cream Cheese Frosting

¼ *cup butter, room temperature*
1 8-ounce package cream cheese, room temperature
1 16-ounce box powdered sugar
1 teaspoon vanilla extract
1 tablespoon cream (if necessary)

Cream butter and cream cheese together. Add powdered sugar. Beat until smooth. Add vanilla; continue beating until vanilla is mixed into frosting. Add cream to thin, if necessary. Spread on cooled cake.

Plaid Tartan

8 rolls fruit leather strips, 3 colors
powdered sugar

Unroll fruit leather strips. Cut 5 strips of fruit leather 18 inches long. Lay them out horizontally on cutting board or countertop side by side, alternating different colors. Cut the remaining fruit leather into 18 5-inch strips. With 1 short strip, begin weaving the fruit leather by placing the short strip over and under the longer strips from the center of the longer strips. It will be necessary to lift the ends of the longer strips back in order to weave the fruit leather—similar to weaving a lattice pie crust. Weave from the center to the right end and then from the center to the left end. Make sure to keep all pieces tightly woven with no spaces between them vertically or horizontally. Trim the edges with a rotary "pizza" cutter or sharp knife. Gently lift the tartan and place it diagonally across the frosted cake.

At the scene of the Gathering Qwilleran and Polly climbed to the top of the bleachers to ensure the best view. First there were the marching bands, featuring bagpipes and drums and representing the counties of Lockmaster and Bixby.

"The very sound of a bagpipe-and-drum band makes me teary-eyed with Scottish pride," Polly said.

Qwilleran admitted that he liked the sound but was not moved to tears. (**Robbed a Bank**)

Chocolate Shortbread Fingers

1 cup butter, softened
½ cup sugar
2 cups all-purpose flour
⅛ teaspoon salt
2 2-ounce squares dipping chocolate

Cream butter and sugar. Gradually add flour and salt. Chill 1 hour. Preheat oven to 325 degrees. On a floured surface, roll dough into a rectangle ½ inch in thickness. Cut horizontally into 12 strips and then vertically down the middle to make 24 strips of dough. With floured hands, roll each strip into a "finger." Place on an ungreased cookie sheet. Bake for 20 minutes until edges are slightly browned. Cool for 5 minutes and then remove cookies to a cooling rack. Cool completely. Melt chocolate according to package directions. Dip one end of each cookie in chocolate and place on wax paper to cool. Chill to set chocolate. MAKES 2 DOZEN.

The final event was the pibroch, performed by the police chief of Pickax. The centuries-old tradition called for a lone piper to play a succession of pieces increasing in difficulty, all the while walking slowly about the stage. For the piper it was a challenge; for the audience it was a mesmerizing experience, almost spiritual in its effect. The crowd watched in total silence. Polly claimed to have been in a trance.

Qwilleran said, "In the Scottish community Andy is considered the master of the pibroch."
(Robbed a Bank)

Nance's Blackberry Crumble

2 12-ounce packages frozen blackberries (or 5 cups fresh blackberries)
½ cup sugar
2 tablespoons + 1 cup all-purpose flour
⅔ cup rolled oats
½ cup brown sugar, firmly packed
½ cup butter

Preheat oven to 375 degrees. Place berries in a buttered 9-inch-square baking dish and sprinkle with sugar and 2 tablespoons flour. In a small bowl mix together 1 cup flour, rolled oats, brown sugar, and butter. Spread crumb mixture evenly over blackberries. Bake for 45 minutes or until top is crisp. Serve with Dorothy's Homemade Vanilla Ice Cream (page 85). SERVES 6

Dorothy's Homemade Vanilla Ice Cream

---

4 cups milk
2 cups sugar
dash salt
4 cups half-and-half
2 teaspoons vanilla extract

Place milk in large saucepan and heat over low heat until milk is scalded (150 degrees). Remove from heat and stir in sugar and salt. Stir until sugar dissolves. Add half-and-half and vanilla. Refrigerate until chilled. Place mixture in ice cream maker and follow manufacturer's directions for freezing ice cream. SERVES 10–12.

Chocolate Chocolate Chip Cookies

⅔ cup shortening
1 cup brown sugar, firmly packed
1 cup sugar
3 eggs
2 cups all-purpose flour
½ cup cocoa
1 teaspoon baking powder
½ teaspoon salt
1 teaspoon vanilla extract
1 cup chocolate chips

Preheat oven to 350 degrees. Cream shortening and sugars. Beat in eggs. Mix together the flour, cocoa, baking powder, and salt in a separate bowl. Beat flour mixture into creamed mixture. Stir in vanilla and chocolate chips. Drop by rounded tablespoonfuls onto cookie sheets. Bake 12–14 minutes. MAKES 3–4 DOZEN COOKIES.

The walls of the lower lounge [of the Scottish Lodge] were covered with maps, photographs of Scotland, and swatches of clan tartans. Qwilleran found the Mackintosh dress tartan, mostly red, and the Mackintosh dress tartan, mostly green for camouflage in the woods. (**Tailed a Thief**)

Suddenly the music stopped, the lights blinked for attention, and a bagpiper swaggered into the [Scottish] hall playing Scotland the Brave. He was Andrew Brodie, the police chief, doing what he liked best. (**Robbed a Bank**)

Goodwinter Family Reunion

The Annual Goodwinter Gathering
Old Stone Church Basement Fellowship Hall
Park Circle
August 18
6:00
Bring a covered dish to share
for our potluck supper.

Family photos will be collected to add to
the Goodwinter Album.

Entertainment to follow.

"Should I know what a covered dish is?" Qwilleran asked innocently.

"Why, it's a dish to pass at a potluck supper!" Carol informed him. *"Don't you go to potluck suppers?"* (**Robbed a Bank**)

Beverage and Bread

Spiced Mocha Coffee

½ pint whipping cream
3 tablespoons powdered sugar
½ teaspoon + ½ teaspoon cinnamon
½ teaspoon nutmeg
8 cups strong, hot coffee
8 teaspoons chocolate syrup

Beat whipping cream until soft peaks form; add sugar, ½ teaspoon cinnamon, and nutmeg. Stir ½ teaspoon cinnamon into coffee. Place 1 teaspoon chocolate syrup each into 8 cups. Add coffee; stir to incorporate syrup. Top with whipped cream. Serves 8.

Onion Bread

2 tablespoons + ⅓ cup soft butter
1½ cups chopped onion
2 cups all-purpose flour
2 teaspoons baking powder
1 teaspoon salt
2 tablespoons dried parsley flakes
1 egg
1 cup milk
½ cup grated fresh Parmesan cheese
paprika

Preheat oven to 425 degrees. Heat 2 tablespoons butter in small skillet. Add onion and cook over medium heat, stirring until onions are tender. Mix flour, baking powder, salt, parsley, and 2 tablespoons cooked onions. Incorporate ⅓ cup butter into flour mixture. Add egg and milk. Stir until blended. Spread into 8×8-inch baking pan. Place remaining onions over top of batter. Sprinkle with cheese and paprika. Bake 30 minutes. Serves 8.

"Let me explain the Goodwinter family," said Qwilleran. There are forty-nine of them in the latest Pickax phone book, all descended from four brothers. There are the much-admired Goodwinters, like Doctor Halifax, and the eccentric Goodwinters, like . . . Amanda. Another branch of the family specializes in black sheep, or so it would seem. But the unfortunate Goodwinters that your mother [Iris Cobb] mentioned are all the progeny of the eldest brother, Ephraim. He jinxed his whole line of descendents."

"How did he do that?" [asked Dennis]

"He was greedy. He owned the Goodwinter Mine and the local newspaper and a couple of banks in the county, but he was too stingy to provide safety measures for the mine. The result was an explosion that killed thirty-two miners." (**Talked to Ghosts**)

Junior Goodwinter had a boyish face and a boyish build and was growing a beard in an attempt to look older than fifteen. (**Talked to Ghosts**)

Salads and Side Dishes

Pineapple-Cantaloupe Salad

1 3-ounce package pineapple gelatin
1 cup boiling water
1 8-ounce can crushed pineapple, undrained
2 cups fresh cantaloupe balls
¾ cup sour cream
3 tablespoons sugar
¼ teaspoon ground ginger

𝕸𝖎𝖝 gelatin and water, stirring until gelatin is dissolved. Stir in pineapple. Cool. Add cantaloupe. Chill until set. Mix sour cream, sugar, and ginger. Top gelatin with ginger-cream mixture. Serves 4–6.

Alexander [Goodwinter] and his sister Penelope . . . shared the patrician features and blond hair characteristic of Goodwinters. . . [They were] a tall impressive pair with . . . an elegant presence. (**Played Post Office**)

Special Days Fruit Salad

2 eggs, beaten
5 tablespoons lemon juice
2 tablespoons butter
3 tablespoons sugar
½ pound marshmallows
1 8-ounce can crushed pineapple, drained
1 banana, sliced
1 8¼-ounce can mandarin oranges, drained
⅓ cup pecans, chopped
½ pint whipping cream

Place eggs in double boiler. Add lemon juice, butter, sugar, and marshmallows. Cook and stir constantly over low heat until marshmallows are melted. Remove from heat and cool. Add pineapple, banana, mandarin oranges, and pecans. Whip cream and fold into fruit mixture before it has completely set. Pour into serving dish. Chill several hours. SERVES 6.

Pamela's Peachy Salad

1 3-ounce package peach gelatin
1 16-ounce container small-curd cottage cheese
1 15¼-ounce can peach chunks, drained
1 8-ounce container nondairy whipped topping

Stir dry gelatin into cottage cheese; mix well. Add peaches; fold in whipped topping. Chill before serving. SERVES 6.

They were passing through farm country, and he [Qwilleran] asked Junior if he knew a potato farmer named Gil Inchpot.

"Not personally, but his daughter was my date for the senior prom in high school. She was the only girl short enough for me."

"You're no longer short, Junior. You're what they call vertically challenged."

"Gee, thanks! That makes me feel nine feet tall." (**Went into the Closet**)

Rice-Bean Salad

1 15½-ounce can kidney beans
2 hardboiled eggs
1 cup cooked rice
½ cup sweet pickle relish
¼ cup chopped onion
¼ cup chopped celery
¼ cup chopped green pepper
½ teaspoon salt
¼ teaspoon pepper
⅓ cup mayonnaise
lettuce or mixed greens

Drain and rinse kidney beans. Place in large bowl. Chop eggs and add to beans along with remaining ingredients except the lettuce. Stir gently. Place in refrigerator to chill. Serve on lettuce. SERVES 6–8.

At a restaurant in Middle Hummock he tried to phone Junior, but there was no answer at Grandma Gage's house. Upon arriving home, he [Qwilleran] discovered why. There was a message on the answering machine. "Hi! We're [Junior Goodwinter and Jody] flying Down Below to get married. Jody's parents live near Cleveland. Hope we get back before the snow flies. And hey! They found Dad's lockbox." (**Knew Shakespeare**)

WPKX went on the air with more storm news, good and bad: "The first baby born during the Big Snow is a seven-pound girl, Leslie Ann. The parents are Mr. and Mrs. Junior Goodwinter. Mother and child are snowbound at the Pickax Hospital." (**Went into the Closet**)

Lima-Bacon Salad

4 slices bacon
2 15¼-ounce can lima beans
4 tablespoons finely chopped onion
2 small tomatoes
4 tablespoons mayonnaise
2 teaspoons apple cider vinegar
½ teaspoon salt
lettuce

Fry bacon and dice. Place in bowl. Drain and rinse lima beans and add to bacon. Chop tomatoes and add to mixture. Mix mayonnaise, vinegar, and salt. Stir into bean-bacon mixture. Chill for several hours. Serve on lettuce. SERVES 6–8.

He [Qwilleran] sank into his lounge chair, propping both feet on the ottoman and thought about Moose County . . . and about Melinda Goodwinter's wicked green eyes and long lashes. . . . Melinda, for her part, had a youthful appeal that he had once found irresistible, and she had a way of asking for what she wanted. (**Moved a Mountain***)*

Parmesan Potato Wedges

6 potatoes, with skins on
½ cup butter
⅔ cup all-purpose flour
¼ cup fresh grated Parmesan cheese
1 teaspoon salt
1 teaspoon dried basil
¼ teaspoon pepper

Preheat oven to 375 degrees. Wash potatoes. Cut each potato into 8 wedges; place wedges in bowl of water until all potatoes are cut. Melt butter in oven in 9×13-inch baking dish. In plastic bag, combine flour, cheese, salt, basil, and pepper. Pat potatoes dry. Shake a few at a time in flour mixture; arrange in single layer in the butter. Bake, uncovered, for 30 minutes. Turn potatoes and bake an additional 30 minutes. Serves 8.

Corn Pudding

4 14¾-ounce cans cream-style corn
⅔ cup all-purpose flour
4 cups milk
⅔ cup sugar
½ cup melted butter
8 eggs, well-beaten
2 teaspoons salt
½ teaspoon pepper

Preheat oven to 375 degrees. Mix corn and flour. Stir in milk, sugar, and butter. Add eggs, salt, and pepper. Mix well. Pour into buttered 3-quart baking dish. Bake for 40–45 minutes or until knife inserted in center comes out clean. SERVES 12.

Squash Casserole

---

1 pound zucchini squash
½ pound yellow crookneck squash
½ cup chopped onion
2 cups shredded Cheddar cheese
½ cup evaporated milk
¼ cup water, drained from squash
¼ teaspoon pepper
¾ cup crushed cracker crumbs
3 tablespoons melted butter

*P*reheat oven to 350 degrees. Slice zucchini and yellow squash. Cook squash and onion in 3 cups boiling salted water for 5 minutes or until tender. Drain, reserving ¼ cup water. Alternate layers of zucchini, yellow squash, and cheese in 1½-quart casserole. Combine milk with squash water and pepper. Pour over layers of vegetables and cheese. Bake for 25 minutes. Remove from oven and top with mixture of crackers and butter. Bake for an additional 10 minutes or until crackers are golden brown. SERVES 4–6.

"Next Qwilleran called Junior Goodwinter at home and said, "You left a message on my machine. What's on your mind?"

"I have news for you, Qwill. Grandma Gage is here from Florida to sign the house over to me. Are you still interested in renting?"

"Definitely." Now Qwilleran was even more eager to live on the property where Polly had her carriage house. (**Wasn't There**)

"Why was I dumb enough to let Grandma Gage unload that white elephant on me?" Junior complained. "She just wanted to avoid paying taxes and insurance, and now I'm stuck with all the bills. If I could find a buyer, I'd let the place go for peanuts, but who wants to live in a castle? People like ranch houses with sliding glass doors and smoke detectors." (**Went into the Closet**)

Green Bean Casserole

-----

2 pounds frozen French-style green beans
1 pound fresh sliced mushrooms
1 medium onion, finely chopped
6 tablespoons butter
4 tablespoons all-purpose flour
2 cups milk
2 5-ounce jars sharp pasteurized process cheese spread
2 tablespoons Worcestershire sauce
2 5-ounce cans sliced water chestnuts, drained
½ cup slivered almonds

Cook green beans according to package directions; drain. Saute mushrooms and onion in butter in large saucepan. Add flour, stirring until smooth. Add milk, cheese spread, and Worcestershire sauce. Stir until cheese melts. Add green beans, water chestnuts, and almonds. Simmer 5 minutes. SERVES 12.

Corn Relish

-----

4 cups fresh or frozen corn
½ cup chopped green pepper
¼ cup chopped red sweet pepper
1¼ cups chopped cabbage
¼ cup chopped onion
1½ teaspoons salt
1½ teaspoons mustard seed
1½ teaspoons celery seed

1½ teaspoons turmeric
1 cup cider vinegar
¼ cup water
½ cup sugar

If using frozen corn, cook according to package directions. If using fresh corn, cook on cob about 5 minutes before cutting from cob. Add all the remaining ingredients to the drained corn. Bring to a boil; simmer 15 minutes. Chill. MAKES APPROXIMATELY 4 CUPS.

Meats

"I remember Pug when she used to come into the library for books on horses; she married a rancher. Jack went into advertising; he was always a very clever boy." [said Polly] (**Went into the Closet**)

"What will you do with your antiques when you move?" Qwilleran asked innocently.
"Sell them at auction. Do you like auctions? They're a major pastime in Moose County— next to potluck suppers and messing around." [answered Gritty]
"Oh, Mother!" Pug remonstrated. She turned to Qwilleran. *"That big rolltop desk belonged to my great-grandfather. He founded the* Picayune. (**Knew Shakespeare**)

Pug's Curry Chicken Salad

3 cups cooked, chopped chicken
1 cup diced celery
1 cup halved seedless grapes
½ cup chopped pecans
¾ cup light mayonnaise
¼ cup whipping cream, whipped
½ teaspoon curry powder or to taste
¼ teaspoon salt
⅛ teaspoon pepper

Cool chicken and combine with celery, grapes, and pecans. Mix mayonnaise, whipped cream, curry powder, salt, and pepper. Pour over chicken mixture. Mix well. Chill. SERVES 6.

"Gritty liked the country club life—golf, cards, dinner dances. I wanted her to serve on my board of trustees, but it was too dull for her taste." [Polly said.]

"Gritty? Is that Mrs. Goodwinter's name?" [asked Quilleran.]

"Gertrude, actually, but there's a certain clique here that clings to their adolescent nicknames: Muffy, Buffy, Bunky, Dodo. I must admit that Mrs. Goodwinter has an abundance of grit, for good or ill. She's like her mother; Euphonia Gage is a spunky woman." (**Knew Shakespeare**)

Gritty's Saucy Deviled Eggs

6 hardboiled eggs
¼ cup finely chopped onions
1 tablespoon + ⅓ cup butter
3 thin slices boiled ham
3 tablespoons mayonnaise
1 teaspoon spicy brown mustard
1 teaspoon Worcestershire sauce
3 tablespoons all-purpose flour
2 cups milk

Preheat oven to 350 degrees. Remove shells from eggs. Cut eggs lengthwise. Remove yolks. Saute onions in 1 tablespoon butter. Finely chop ham in food processor. Mix yolks, onions, ham, mayonnaise, mustard, and Worcestershire sauce. Fill egg whites with yolk mixture. Place in buttered casserole. Melt ⅓ cup butter in saucepan. Stir flour into butter. Slowly add milk, stirring constantly over medium heat until sauce thickens. Gently pour over eggs. Bake 15–20 minutes or until eggs are heated through. SERVES 6.

Meat Loaf

2 pounds lean ground beef
¾ cup fine, dry bread crumbs
1 egg
½ small onion, finely chopped
2 teaspoons seasoning salt
¼ teaspoon pepper
2 teaspoons Worcestershire sauce
½ cup ketchup

Preheat oven to 350 degrees. Mix ground beef, bread crumbs, and egg together in large bowl. Add onion, salt, pepper, Worcestershire sauce, and ketchup. Mix well. Shape into oval mound and place in casserole dish or roasting pan. Bake 1½ hours or until temperature in center of loaf reaches 170 degrees. SERVES 8.

"Qwill, I want to thank you for buying my dad's [Dr. Halifax] paintings." [said Melinda]
"Don't thank me. The K Foundation purchased them for exhibition."
"But you must have instigated the deal. At a hundred dollars apiece it came to $101,500. Foxy Fred would have sold them for a thousand dollars." (**Wasn't There**)

Michael's Favorite Steak Roll-Ups

1½ pounds round steak
½ teaspoon salt
⅛ teaspoon pepper
⅔ cup water
2 tablespoons butter
2 cups packaged herb-seasoned stuffing mix
8 baby carrots, cut into strips
4 celery strips approximately 2½ inches long
4 small onion wedges
toothpicks
¼ cup all-purpose flour
oil
1 14-ounce can beef broth
½ cup sour cream

Preheat oven to 325 degrees. Cut meat into 4 pieces. If necessary, pound out to about ¼ inch in thickness. Sprinkle with salt and pepper. Set aside. Bring water and butter to a boil. Remove from heat. Add stuffing mix and stir with fork until moist throughout. Place approximately ½ cup stuffing near center of each piece of meat. Place 2 carrot strips, 1 celery strip, and 1 onion wedge on top of stuffing. Roll meat, fasten with toothpicks. Roll in flour; brown in oil in hot skillet. Place in casserole dish. Add beef broth. Bake, covered, 1½ hours or until meat is tender. Remove meat from dish. Stir sour cream into liquid in casserole to make gravy. Remove toothpicks from meat; place meat in gravy. SERVES 4.

Nick's Pork Chops

---

4 apples
8 pork chops, about ½ inch thick
3–4 tablespoons oil
½ teaspoon salt
½ teaspoon sage
¼ cup brown sugar, firmly packed
2 tablespoons all-purpose flour
1 cup hot water
1 tablespoon vinegar
½ cup raisins

Preheat oven to 350 degrees. Peel, core, and slice apples. Brown chops in oil. Place in baking dish. Sprinkle with salt and sage. Top with apple slices; sprinkle with sugar. Stir flour into oil in skillet where chops were browned; add water and vinegar. Cook until mixture thickens. Add raisins and pour over pork chops. Bake uncovered, 60 minutes. SERVES 8.

Tuna Casserole

---

1 6-ounce can solid white tuna, drained
1 10¾-ounce can cream of chicken soup
1 8-ounce can sliced water chestnuts, drained
1 4-ounce can sliced mushrooms, drained
⅓ cup cashews, chopped
½ cup finely sliced celery
⅓ cup chopped onion
2 cups chow mein noodles
⅓ cup water

Preheat oven to 350 degrees. Combine tuna and soup. Stir in water chestnuts, mushrooms, cashews, celery, onion, noodles, and water. Place in buttered 1½-quart casserole. Bake 30–35 minutes. SERVES 6.

Kielbasa and Corn Bread Pie

7 ounces kielbasa sausage
1 small onion, coarsely chopped
½ cup coarsely chopped green pepper pieces
2 tablespoons tomato paste
⅓ cup water
½ cup all-purpose flour
½ cup cornmeal
1 tablespoon sugar
¼ teaspoon salt
½ tablespoon baking powder
1 egg
½ cup milk
1 tablespoon melted butter

Preheat oven to 425 degrees. Cut sausage into 1-inch pieces and place in a skillet. Add onions and peppers. Cook over medium heat until onions and peppers are soft and meat is browned. Add tomato paste and water. Simmer for 10 minutes. In a small bowl mix flour, cornmeal, sugar, salt, and baking powder. In a separate bowl whisk together egg, milk, and butter; add to cornmeal mixture. Place batter in a greased 8-inch pie pan. Pour the sausage mixture in the middle of the cornmeal batter. Bake for 15–20 minutes or until toothpick inserted in corn bread comes out clean. SERVES 6.

Chicken-Rice Casserole

5 cups cooked, diced chicken
1 cup cooked rice
¼ cup finely chopped onion
½ teaspoon paprika
1 teaspoon salt
4 eggs
3 cups milk

Preheat oven to 375 degrees. Mix chicken, rice, and onion together. Stir in paprika and salt. Beat eggs and milk together. Pour over chicken mixture. Stir well. Place in greased casserole. Bake 45 minutes or until knife inserted in center comes out clean. Top with Chicken Sauce. SERVES 6–8.

Chicken Sauce

1 10¾-ounce can cream of chicken soup
1 cup sour cream
¼ cup drained diced pimiento

Mix all ingredients. Heat over low heat. Serve with Chicken-Rice Casserole.

Desserts

Across from the doctor's residence there was another stone mansion that Amanda Goodwinter had inherited from her branch of the family, and when Qwilleran arrived on the scene she was standing on her porch with hands on hips, glaring at the mob. "The city council will act on this at our next meeting!" she declared when she saw him. "We'll pass an ordinance against disrupting peaceful neighborhoods with commercial activities! I don't care that she's [Melinda] my cousin and a doctor and an orphan! This can't be allowed! She's a selfish brat and always has been!" (**Wasn't There**)

Melinda's Minties

1 cup chopped walnuts
1½ cups miniature marshmallows
4 cups graham cracker crumbs
1 cup powdered sugar
1 12-ounce package semisweet chocolate pieces
1 cup evaporated milk
1 teaspoon peppermint extract

Mix walnuts, marshmallows, cracker crumbs, and sugar in large mixing bowl. Heat chocolate pieces and milk in a small saucepan over low heat. Stir constantly until smooth. Remove from heat and stir in peppermint extract. Reserve ½ cup of chocolate mixture. Mix remaining chocolate mixture with cracker mixture. Stir well. Place in a buttered 9x9-inch pan. Press down. Spread remaining chocolate mixture on top. Chill. Cut into squares. MAKES 16 SQUARES.

At two-thirty he rang the doorbell of a large stone house on Goodwinter Boulevard, to interview the eighty-two-year-old president of the Old Timers Club. The woman who came to the door was the right age, but he [Qwilleran] doubted that she could do headstands and push-ups.

"Mrs. Gage is in her studio," the woman said. "You can go right in—through the front parlor."

A gloomy cave of dark velvet, heavy carved furniture, and black horsehair upholstery led into a light, bright studio, unfurnished except for two large mirrors and an exercise mat. A little woman in leotard, tights, and leg warmers sat in lotus position on the mat. She rose effortlessly and came forward. She was petite but not frail, white-haired but smooth-skinned.

(Knew Shakespeare)

. . . "she [Grandma Gage] drove a Mercedes at twenty miles an hour and blew the horn at every intersection. [said Lyle] The police were always ticketing her for obstructing traffic. All the Gages have been a little batty, although Junior seems to have his head on straight."

(Went into the Closet)

Grandma Gage's Washboard Cookies

1 cup shortening
1 cup sugar
1 cup brown sugar, firmly packed
1 cup creamy peanut butter
2 eggs
4 cups all-purpose flour
2 teaspoons baking soda
1 teaspoon salt

Preheat oven to 375 degrees. Cream shortening, sugars, and peanut butter. Add eggs. Beat well. Mix flour, baking soda, and salt together. Add to peanut butter mixture. Mix thoroughly. Shape into log in wax paper about 12 inches long and 1½ inches in diameter. Flatten all 4 sides to make a long "square." Cut into ¼-inch slices. Place on greased cookie sheet. Using fork tines, make indentations like an old-fashioned washboard. Bake 8–10 minutes. MAKES 8 DOZEN.

Graham Cracker Pie

3 egg whites
1 cup sugar
1 teaspoon vanilla extract
1 cup graham cracker crumbs
½ teaspoon baking powder
½ cup chopped pecans

Preheat oven to 350 degrees. Beat egg whites until stiff. Fold in sugar, vanilla, cracker crumbs, baking powder, and pecans. Place in greased 9-inch pie plate. Bake for 30 minutes. Remove from oven and cool. SERVES 6.

Boiled Cookies

½ *cup butter*
½ *cup milk*
1 *teaspoon vanilla*
¼ *cup cocoa*
2 *cups sugar*
½ *cup creamy peanut butter*
3 *cups quick-cooking oatmeal*
½ *cup chopped pecans*

Place butter, milk, vanilla, cocoa, and sugar in a saucepan; bring to a boil over medium heat. Boil for 1 minute; remove from heat. Add peanut butter, oatmeal, and nuts; mix well. Drop by teaspoonfuls onto waxed paper; cool. MAKES 5 DOZEN COOKIES.

"Penelope still eats ice cream with a fork. Socially she was a throwback to the Edwardian era. [Melinda said] My great-grandmother owned sixteen etiquette books. In those days people didn't worry about losing weight or getting in touch with their feelings; they wanted to know if they should eat mashed potatoes with a knife."

They went to Melinda's condo to look at her great-grandmother's etiquette books, and Qwilleran arrived home at a late hour, humming a tune from The Student Prince. (**Played Post Office**)

Penelope's Old-Fashioned Peach-Almond Ice Cream

---

2 *cups milk*
2 *cups sliced fresh peaches*
1 *cup sugar*

3 cups half-and-half
1 teaspoon vanilla extract
1 cup sliced almonds

Scald milk (150 degrees) in small saucepan; cool. Use a hand blender or food processor to puree peaches with sugar. When milk is cool, add peach mixture, half-and-half, vanilla, and almonds. Refrigerate until chilled. Place mixture in ice cream maker and follow manufacturer's directions for freezing ice cream. SERVES 8.

[Amanda Goodwinter] was a scowling gray-haired woman. [She wears] baggy dresses and thick-soled shoes. (**Played Post Office**)

"The major event will be the ribbon-cutting, with Mayor Amanda Goodwinter wearing her usual scarecrow clothing and putting on her usual bad-tempered act." [said Dwight Somers] (**Went Bananas**)

"Say, I'm all excited about your party. Hope you've got some good bourbon." [said Amanda.] (**Played Post Office**)

Amanda's Bourbon Balls

1 cup + ½ cup powdered sugar
¼ cup bourbon whiskey
2 tablespoons light corn syrup
2½ cups finely crushed chocolate graham crackers or chocolate wafers
1 cup finely chopped pecans

Mix 1 cup powdered sugar, bourbon, and corn syrup. Add graham cracker crumbs and pecans; mix thoroughly. Let stand 15 minutes. Form small balls about 1 inch in diameter. Roll in ½ cup powdered sugar. MAKES 3½ TO 4 DOZEN.

Rich Chocolate Cake

4 squares unsweetened baking chocolate
¾ cup butter
2 eggs
2 cups sugar
2 cups all-purpose flour
½ cup milk
1½ teaspoons baking soda
1½ cups boiling water

Preheat oven to 350 degrees. Melt chocolate and butter in small saucepan. Mix eggs and sugar together. Blend flour and milk into egg mixture. Add chocolate mixture. Mix baking soda and boiling water. Pour hot water and baking soda into flour mixture in a thin stream, stirring constantly. Put batter into greased, floured 9×13-inch pan. Bake 30–35 minutes or until center of cake springs back when pressed lightly. Cool completely. Frost cake when cooled. SERVES 12.

Frosting
4 cups powdered sugar
1 cup marshmallow cream
½ cup butter, softened
3–4 tablespoons milk
1 teaspoon vanilla extract

Mix sugar, marshmallow cream, and butter together. Add milk and vanilla. Spread frosting on cooled cake.

Riker—Hanstable Friends Reunion

Dear Family of Friends,

Friends we have many.
With family we've been blessed.
But when friends are like family
We consider that the best.

Join us for a Lakeside Luau at Sunny Daze to toast the warm friendships we have enjoyed for so many years. Arch will provide the drinks and Mildred will prepare the meats. Please come and bring your favorite Hawaiian side dish or dessert on August 7 at 6:00.

Arch and Mildred

Qwilleran set out on the half-mile walk to Mildred's place. A desolate stretch of beach bordered his own property, lapped by languid waves. Next, an outcropping of rock projected into the water, popularly known as Seagull Point, although one rarely saw a gull unless the lake washed up a dead fish . . . A flight of twenty wooden steps led up the side of the dune to Mildred's terrace. (**Went Underground**)

Beverages and Bread

Blue Hawaii

1 ounce light rum
1 ounce blue Curaçao
4 ounces pineapple juice
2 ounces orange juice
3 ounces ice

Combine all ingredients, except ice. Shake and strain over ice in hurricane glass. Garnish with pineapple, if desired.

Arch was always quick with a toast. "Here's to old friends who know you well but still like you!" (**Robbed a Bank**)

Piña Colada

2 ounces light rum
2 ounces coconut cream
4 ounces pineapple juice
½ cup crushed ice

Pour all ingredients over ½ cup ice in blender. Blend well. Serve in collins glass. Garnish with cherry and add umbrella straw, if desired.

Tropical Breeze Freeze

2 cups sugar
2 cups water
4 navel oranges, juiced
3 lemons, juiced
2 bananas, sliced
1 8-ounce can crushed pineapple, undrained
8 cups cracked ice
½ cup water or ¼ cup water and 2 ounces light rum

Place sugar and water in saucepan. Stir over medium heat until sugar dissolves. Cool. Blend orange juice, lemon juice, bananas, and pineapple in food processor or blender. Freeze in eight 1-cup plastic containers. When ready to use, remove juice from 1 container and place in blender with 1 cup cracked ice and water. Blend on high speed. Repeat to make 7 more 16-ounce drinks. SERVES 8.

Luau Brew

4 cups milk
1 3½-ounce can sweetened shredded coconut
4 cups brewed coffee, hot

Preheat oven to 350 degrees. Place milk and coconut in a saucepan. Bring to a boil; reduce heat and simmer for 8 minutes. Strain milk to separate coconut and milk. Place coconut on an ungreased cookie sheet. Bake coconut until golden brown; approximately 10 minutes. Mix coffee and milk together. Garnish with toasted coconut. SERVES 6–8.

Sweet Potato Loaf

2 cups sugar
1½ cups cooking oil
3 eggs
2 cups cooked mashed sweet potatoes
1 cup crushed pineapple, undrained
3¼ cups all-purpose flour
1 teaspoon cinnamon
1 teaspoon nutmeg
½ teaspoon salt
1 teaspoon baking soda
1 cup chopped pecans

Preheat oven to 350 degrees. Grease and flour 2 5×9-inch loaf pans. Cream sugar and oil together. Add eggs, one at a time. Add sweet potatoes, pineapple, flour, cinnamon, nutmeg, salt, and baking soda. Mix well; add pecans. Pour into prepared loaf pans. Bake 50–55 minutes or until toothpick comes out clean when inserted into center of loaf. SERVES 12.

"Guests were gathering there, all wearing dark glasses, which gave them a certain anonymity. They were a colorful crew—in beach dresses, sailing stripes, clamdiggers and halters, raw-hued espadrilles, sandals, Indian prints, Hawaiian shirts, and peasant blouses. Even Lyle Compton, the superintendent of schools, was wearing a daring pair of plaid trousers." (**Went Underground**)

Salads and Side Dishes

Hawaiian Outrigger with Coconut Dip

2 cups milk
1 6-ounce package frozen flaked coconut
1 tablespoon cornstarch
3 tablespoons sugar
assorted fresh fruit of choice
1 large watermelon
12 12-inch bamboo skewers

Combine milk and coconut. Bring to boil over low heat, stirring frequently. Remove from heat and let stand 20 minutes; stir several times. Strain, reserve milk; discard coconut. Combine cornstarch and sugar in saucepan. Add ½ cup coconut milk, blending well. Add remaining coconut milk to cornstarch mixture, stirring constantly over medium heat until thickened. Refrigerate until cool.

Cut watermelon in shape of Hawaiian longboat with low sides and tall prow. Use a melon ball tool to scoop out flesh of watermelon. Set balls aside in refrigerator. Using a small paring knife or pumpkin carving tool, make circular holes in sides near top of watermelon "boat." Insert 6 skewers on each side below holes slanting toward "water" to represent oars. Mix watermelon balls with other bite-sized pieces of assorted fruits; place in watermelon "boat." Serve with coconut dip. Place coconut dip serving dish on ice to keep chilled. SERVES 12.

Polly's Carrot-Raisin Salad

4 cups grated carrots
1 cup raisins
1 8-ounce can pineapple tidbits, drained, 2 tablespoons syrup reserved
1 teaspoon grated gingerroot (or to taste)
⅔ cup mayonnaise

Combine carrots, raisins, and pineapple. Mix gingerroot, mayonnaise, and 2 tablespoons pineapple juice. Blend into carrot mixture. Chill before serving. SERVES 6–8.

Shell Salad

4 cups dry seashell macaroni
⅓ cup olive oil
½ cup finely chopped macadamia nuts
½ cup fresh, shredded Parmesan cheese
¾ cup fresh, chopped basil leaves
1 tablespoon cider vinegar
2 cloves garlic, chopped
¼ teaspoon salt
3 medium tomatoes, chopped

Cook macaroni according to package directions; drain and place in bowl. Make dressing by processing the oil, nuts, cheese, basil, vinegar, garlic, and salt in food processor until thick. Pour dressing over macaroni; add tomatoes and mix well. Chill. SERVES 6.

Only old friends can be invited to dinner at the last minute, and the Rikers were friends of long standing, and no minute was ever too late for a dinner invitation. Arch Riker, now the publisher of the Moose County Something, *had grown up with Qwilleran in Chicago. Mildred Riker, a native of Moose County and now food editor for the paper, had the kind of comfortable, outgoing personality that made new friends feel like old friends.* (**Went Up the Creek**)

Plantains

1 cup all-purpose flour
2 tablespoons brown sugar, firmly packed
1 teaspoon baking powder
pinch salt
½ cup milk
5 ripe (black-skinned) plantains
⅓ cup sugar
½ teaspoon cinnamon
butter
oil

Whisk together flour, sugar, baking powder, salt, and milk to make batter. Peel plantains and cut into diagonal slices ½ inch thick. Mix sugar and cinnamon together; place on a plate. Heat butter and oil in large skillet. Dip plantain slices in batter and fry until golden brown on both sides. Drain on paper towels and coat with sugar-cinnamon mixture while still warm. SERVES 12.

Orange Dream Salad

1 3-ounce package orange gelatin
1 3-ounce package lemon gelatin
1 cup boiling water
1 cup orange sherbet, softened
1 16-ounce can mandarin oranges, drained
1 20-ounce can crushed pineapple, drained

Combine gelatins in bowl. Add boiling water to gelatins. Stir until gelatin is dissolved. Mix in softened sherbet. Add oranges and pineapple. Chill several hours. **Serves 8.**

They [Mildred and Arch] were old enough to have grandchildren but young enough to hold hands under the tablecloth. Both had survived marital upheavals, but now the easygoing publisher had married the warm-hearted Mildred Hanstable . . . (**Came to Breakfast**)

Sea Pearls

1 1-pound bag frozen pearl onions
1 cup cream
½ cup chicken broth
½ teaspoon dill or to taste
⅓ cup sliced almonds
½ teaspoon salt

Place onions in a saucepan of water and bring to a boil. Reduce heat and simmer for 10 minutes. Drain. Add rest of ingredients and cook over low heat just until ingredients are heated through. Do not boil. **Serves 6–8.**

Asparagus-Avocado Salad

1 pound fresh asparagus
1 ripe avocado, peeled, cubed
½ medium cucumber, peeled, diced
1 medium zucchini, diced
1 medium tomato, diced
1 small red onion, sliced
2 tablespoons olive oil
2 tablespoons lemon juice
1 tablespoon cider vinegar
1 teaspoon brown mustard
1 clove garlic
½ teaspoon dried basil
¼ teaspoon thyme
¼ teaspoon salt
⅛ teaspoon pepper

Hold asparagus at ends and snap apart to break; stalks will break at appropriate tender point. Discard tough ends. Break tender spears into bite-sized pieces. Microwave, with 3 tablespoons water, for 3 minutes. Plunge into ice water to cool quickly. Drain, place in large bowl with avocado, cucumber, zucchini, tomato, and onion. Place oil, lemon juice, vinegar, mustard, garlic, basil, thyme, salt, and pepper in blender and blend until garlic is minced. Pour over salad. Toss and refrigerate until chilled. SERVES 6.

Pineapple-Rice Salad

3 cups cooked, cooled rice
⅔ cup chopped celery
2 tablespoons chopped onion
¼ cup chopped red pepper
1 8-ounce can crushed pineapple, drained
¾ cup mayonnaise
1 tablespoon lemon juice
½ teaspoon dry mustard
⅛ teaspoon pepper
½ teaspoon salt

Place rice in medium-sized bowl. Add celery, onion, red pepper, and pineapple. In a separate bowl, mix mayonnaise, lemon juice, dry mustard, pepper, and salt together. Pour over rice mixture. Stir well. Chill before serving. SERVES 8.

The [Top o' the Dunes] club was simply a row of cottages overlooking a hundred miles of blue water and bearing names like "Sunny Daze" and "Many Pines" and "No Oaks." The Riker cottage was bright yellow with black shutters and a broad deck cantilevered over the slope of the dune. On the wide top rail of the deck sat Toulouse, a fluffy black-and-white stray who had wandered into Mildred's life. Qwilleran, upon arrival, always stroked Toulouse and told him he was a handsome brute. (**Talked Turkey**)

Lisa's Hawaiian Hash

2 cups miniature marshmallows
1 8-ounce can crushed pineapple, undrained
½ pint whipping cream
3 tablespoons powdered sugar
½ teaspoon vanilla extract
½ cup frozen flaked coconut
10 maraschino cherries

Mix marshmallows and crushed pineapple. Refrigerate overnight. Whip cream until soft peaks form; add sugar and vanilla. Fold coconut and whipped cream into marshmallows and pineapple. Decorate top of hash with cherries. SERVES 4–6.

Mildred said, "Qwill, I'd like to ask you a great favor."
*"It would be a privilege and a pleasure." He could never say no to Mildred; she was so sincere, generous, and good-natured, and she was such a good cook. (**Saw Stars**)*

Roast Pork with Mango-Peach Sauce

1 teaspoon poultry seasoning
½ teaspoon salt
¼ teaspoon pepper
3–3½ pounds pork loin roast
1 cup peeled, chopped fresh mango
½ cup peeled, chopped fresh peach
¾ cup sugar
⅓ cup water
1 tablespoon lemon juice
1 tablespoon butter
½ teaspoon dried, crushed rosemary
½ teaspoon dried, crushed thyme

Preheat oven to 350 degrees. Mix poultry seasoning, salt, and pepper; rub onto roast. Bake until internal temperature of meat reaches 165 degrees, about 1½ hours. Make sauce while meat is roasting by bringing the rest of the ingredients to a boil in a small saucepan. Cool and blend in blender until smooth. If thinner sauce is desired, add water by tablespoonful. Let roast stand 10–12 minutes before slicing. Just before serving, reheat sauce. Pour over sliced pork. SERVES 8.

Tiki-Tiki Meatballs

---

2 pounds lean ground beef
1 cup finely crushed cracker crumbs
½ cup finely chopped onion
½ teaspoon celery salt
¼ teaspoon pepper
⅓ cup oil
2 red peppers, coarsely chopped
1 20-ounce can pineapple chunks, drained
2 14-ounce cans beef broth
4 tablespoons cornstarch
2 teaspoons soy sauce
½ cup vinegar
½ cup sugar

Mix ground beef, cracker crumbs, onion, celery salt, and pepper. Form into meatballs about 1 inch in diameter. Fry in large skillet in about ⅓ cup oil. Remove meatballs to paper towels to drain. Pour excess oil from skillet. Place red pepper, pineapple chunks, and beef broth in skillet. Cook 8 minutes. Mix cornstarch, soy sauce, vinegar, and sugar. After broth mixture has cooked, add cornstarch mixture to broth. Cook until thick. Put meatballs back into skillet and heat through. MAKES APPROXIMATELY 4 DOZEN MEATBALLS.

Mildred's Chicken Bites

3 tablespoons butter
5 tablespoons all-purpose flour
1 cup chicken broth
¼ teaspoon salt
¼ teaspoon pepper
⅛ teaspoon celery salt
dash red pepper
2 cups cooked, finely chopped chicken
1 egg, beaten
¾ cup toasted bread crumbs
oil

𝔐𝔢𝔩𝔱 butter in medium saucepan; stir in flour. Add broth and stir until mixture thickens. Add salt, pepper, celery salt, and red pepper. Add chicken; chill several hours. Shape into balls. Dip into egg, then bread crumbs. Heat oil to 365–375 degrees. Fry chicken until brown. Drain on paper towels. MAKES ABOUT 24.

This year they [the cottages] had been given names, displayed on rustic signs of routed wood. The golfing Mableys called their place THE SAND TRAP. The old Dunfield cottage, said to be haunted, was now LITTLE MANDERLEY. A little frame house called THE LITTLE FRAME HOUSE was understandable when one knew the owners had a picture-framing business. Then there was BAH HUMBUG, which could belong only to the Comptons . . . Last in the row was the Rikers' cottage, a yellow frame bungalow called SUNNY DAZE. (**Saw Stars**)

Polynesian-Style Beef

4 pounds round steak
oil
2 medium onions, chopped
2 cups water
2 20-ounce cans pineapple chunks
1 cup brown sugar, firmly packed
½ cup soy sauce
2 tablespoons vinegar
2 teaspoons ground ginger
2 tablespoons cornstarch
16 ounces fresh mushrooms, stems removed, sliced
2 medium tomatoes

Cut meat into strips, approximately ½×2×¼ inches. (Meat can be frozen for approximately 1 hour to make it easier to cut into strips.) Brown in oil. Add onions and water. Cover and simmer until meat is tender, about an hour. Add more water, if necessary, so meat does not cook dry. Drain pineapple, reserving juice. To make sauce, add water to juice to make 1 cup; mix with brown sugar, soy sauce, vinegar, ginger, and cornstarch; cook until thickened. Add pineapple and mushrooms to tender meat. Add more water, if necessary, and cook for 3 minutes to heat mushrooms and pineapple. Remove skins from tomatoes by putting them into boiling water briefly. Cut into quarters, and add to pineapple-meat mixture. Pour hot sauce over meat mixture. Serve with rice. SERVES 12–16.

"If I do say so myself, I make a memorable stuffed cabbage, but nothing else." [said Arch Riker]

"How come I've known you since kindergarten and never tasted your memorable stuffed cabbage?" [asked Qwilleran] (**Said Cheese**)

Arch's Memorable Stuffed Cabbage

2 pounds lean ground beef
1 cup commercially prepared toasted bread crumbs
½ cup uncooked rice
½ cup finely chopped onion
½ teaspoon salt
⅛ teaspoon pepper
1 large head cabbage
1 16-ounce jar chopped sauerkraut
2 15-ounce cans tomato sauce

Preheat oven to 325 degrees. Mix ground beef, bread crumbs, rice, onion, salt, and pepper. Refrigerate mixture while preparing cabbage leaves. Remove core from cabbage. Run hot water over outer leaves and cut off, one at a time. Place in large pan and boil gently until pliable. Remove from water; cut leaf in half along heavy center vein, removing vein to make rolling easier. Place 1–2 tablespoons meat mixture in center of each half-leaf of cabbage. Roll, tucking ends of cabbage in. Place in large baking pan. Cover each layer of cabbage rolls with chopped sauerkraut and tomato sauce. Cover and bake approximately 2 hours. MAKES 6–8 SERVINGS.

Desserts

The car parked alongside the police vehicles, and Qwilleran recognized Roger MacGillivray's ten-year-old boneshaker. He went out to meet the bearded young man who had given up teaching history in order to report living history for the local paper. (**Knew a Cardinal**)

"What are you doing here?" he [Qwilleran] asked. "Shouldn't you be at home?—home schooling your brats around the kitchen table?"

She was Sharon Hanstable—plump, good-natured, and wholesomely pretty—a young version of her mother, Mildred Riker. She was also wife of Roger MacGillivray, a reporter for The Moose County Something. (**Saw Stars**)

Sharon's Lime Pie

1 8-ounce package cream cheese, softened
4 eggs
1 14-ounce can sweetened condensed milk
⅔ cup fresh lime juice
½ cup sugar
2 drops green food coloring (optional)
1 teaspoon bitters (optional)
2 graham cracker pie shells
1 pint whipping cream
½ teaspoon vanilla extract
5 tablespoons powdered sugar

Preheat oven to 325 degrees. In a mixing bowl, combine cream cheese and eggs. Add condensed milk, lime juice, and sugar. Add food coloring and bitters, if desired. Beat until smooth. Pour into pie shells. Bake 25–30 minutes. Chill before serving. Beat whipping cream until soft peaks form. Stir in vanilla and powdered sugar. Divide whipped cream between the two pies and dollop on top of cooled filling. SERVES 10–12.

Macadamia Nut Cream Pie

¾ cup sugar
½ cup all-purpose flour
2¾ cups milk
3 egg yolks
1 tablespoon butter
1 teaspoon vanilla extract
⅓ cup chopped macadamia nuts
1 commercially prepared pie shell, baked
½ pint whipping cream
3 tablespoons powdered sugar
1 teaspoon vanilla extract

Combine sugar and flour in saucepan; stir while very slowly adding milk. Bring to a boil over medium heat, stirring constantly. Reduce heat; cook and stir 2 minutes more. Remove from heat. Beat egg yolks. Add 1 cup of heated mixture to the egg yolks, stirring in a tablespoonful at a time. Return egg mixture to saucepan. Return saucepan to medium heat. Stir to boiling point; boil 2 minutes. Remove from heat and stir in butter, vanilla, and nuts. Pour into pie shell. Chill several hours. Whip cream until soft peaks form. Add sugar and vanilla. Spread on chilled pie. Top of pie can be decorated with more macadamia nuts, if desired. SERVES 8.

Jeanette's Coconut Cookies

1 cup brown sugar, firmly packed
½ cup butter, room temperature
2 eggs
1 teaspoon vanilla extract
2 cups all-purpose flour
½ teaspoon salt
1 teaspoon baking powder
1 cup canned sweetened flaked coconut
1 cup chopped walnuts

Preheat oven to 350 degrees. Beat brown sugar and butter together until fluffy. Add eggs; beat well. Add vanilla. In a small bowl combine the flour, salt, and baking powder. Stir flour mixture into the sugar mixture and mix thoroughly. Stir in the coconut and walnuts. Drop by rounded teaspoonfuls onto lightly greased cookie sheet. Bake 9–11 minutes. Makes approximately 3 dozen cookies.

Mindy's Absolutely Delicious Cupcakes

2 cups sugar
1 cup butter, room temperature
3 cups all-purpose flour
1 tablespoon baking powder
½ teaspoon salt
1 cup milk
1 teaspoon vanilla extract
6 egg whites

Preheat oven to 350 degrees. Cream sugar and butter. Combine flour, baking powder, and salt. Add flour mixture to sugar mixture, alternating with milk. Add vanilla. In a separate bowl, beat egg whites until stiff; fold into batter. Spoon into greased cupcake pans or pans lined with cupcake papers. Bake 15–18 minutes. Cool and frost. Decorate with Butter Mint Rosebuds and sprinkle with pink sugar decorating crystals. MAKES 30 LARGE CUPCAKES OR 36 SMALLER CUPCAKES.

Frosting

2 16-ounce boxes powdered sugar
1 cup butter, room temperature
2 teaspoons vanilla extract
½ cup cream

Beat sugar, butter, vanilla, and cream together. Add more cream, if necessary, to achieve spreadable consistency. Generously frost cupcakes.

Butter Mint Rosebuds

5 cups powdered sugar
⅓ cup light corn syrup
¼ cup butter, room temperature
½ teaspoon peppermint extract
2 tablespoons heavy cream
2 drops green food coloring
4 drops red food coloring

With a spoon, mix together all ingredients except food coloring in a large bowl. Then knead by hand, pressing ingredients together until a smooth ball is formed. Remove ¼ of the dough; tint it green. Tint the remaining dough pink. Cover all the dough with plastic wrap until ready to use. Remove approximately ⅓ of the pink dough. Roll out to ⅛-inch thickness. Use a sharp knife to cut dough into ½-inch × 3-inch strips. Working quickly, loosely roll each strip jelly-roll-style to resemble a rose. Pinch one end of the roll and flare out the "petals" of the other end by gently pressing them between fingers. Cut long pinched ends off roses. Place roses on waxed paper, allowing them to dry slightly in the air. Repeat, creating buds with other 2 portions of pink dough. Roll the green dough into ⅛-inch thickness. Use a sharp knife to cut small pointed ovals to resemble leaves. Place 3 roses and 2 leaves on each cupcake. MAKES APPROXIMATELY 108 ROSES AND 72 LEAVES.

Pineapple Chess Bars

Crust
¾ cup butter
2 cups all-purpose flour
½ cup sugar

Preheat oven to 350 degrees. Cream together butter, flour, and sugar. Pat into ungreased 9×12-inch pan. Bake for 15–20 minutes or until crust is lightly browned.

Filling
4 eggs
2 cups sugar
¼ cup butter, room temperature
⅓ cup all-purpose flour
1 8-ounce can crushed pineapple, drained
powdered sugar

Mix together eggs and sugar; add butter. Stir in flour until well blended. Fold in pineapple. Spread over crust. Bake for 20–25 minutes or until center is set. Chill. Sprinkle with powdered sugar. SERVES 12.

Banana Marble Dessert

1 3.4-ounce package chocolate cook-and-serve pudding mix
1 3.4-ounce package vanilla cook-and-serve pudding mix
½ pint whipping cream
2 tablespoons brown sugar, firmly packed
1 teaspoon vanilla extract
12 full graham crackers
1 large banana, sliced
½ cup chopped pecans

Cook puddings according to package directions. Chill. Whip whipping cream until soft peaks form. Add brown sugar and vanilla. Fold whipped cream mixture into vanilla pudding. Crush 3 crackers and reserve crumbs. Break remaining crackers into large pieces. Place half of the cracker pieces on the bottom of 8x8-inch dish. Using half of both puddings, place large spoonfuls randomly over the cracker layer. Make second layer of cracker pieces. Place remaining puddings randomly over the crackers. Gently swirl top layer with spoon, creating a marble effect. Mix reserved crumbs and pecans. Sprinkle over top. SERVES 6–8.

There was a spectacular sunset—a ball of fire sinking into the lake and turning it bloodred. Then the mosquitoes swooped in, and the guests went indoors to play cards. (**Went Underground**)

O'Dell–Robinson Reunion

Attached to small burlap bags of tiny Moose County potatoes was this invitation from fun-loving Celia:

Come to a family reunion at the O'Dells' on Pleasant Street August 31 at 1:00 to celebrate our Irish heritage and our love of Moose County.

"Faith and begorra," we'll have more fun if you're there. Bring your favorite Irish food and the recipe to share. There'll be games and contests galore, story and joke telling, and more.

When Celia's package arrived on Tuesday, Qwilleran sank his teeth into a rich nut-filled, chewy chocolate brownie, and he had a vision. He envisioned Celia transplanted to Pickax, baking meat loaf for the cats and brownies for himself, catering parties now and then, laughing a lot. (**Went into the Closet**)

"That nice Mr. O'Dell was there with his daughter. He talked to us in the lobby. Charming Irish accent!" [said Celia] (**Blew the Whistle**)

Beverage and Breads

Irish Coffee

4 cups strong, hot coffee
2 tablespoons orange juice
4 teaspoons sugar
whiskey to taste
8 tablespoons heavy cream

Mix coffee, orange juice, sugar, and whiskey. Pour into 4 warmed Irish whiskey glasses. Pour cream gently on top of coffee. Do not stir. May be doubled or tripled as desired. SERVES 4.

Whole Wheat Bread

2½ cups whole wheat flour
1¼ cups all-purpose flour
3 tablespoons sugar
1 teaspoon baking soda
½ teaspoon salt
½ cup butter, room temperature
1 egg
1¼ cups buttermilk
1 tablespoon melted butter

Preheat oven to 400 degrees. Grease loaf pan and set aside. Mix flours, sugar, baking soda, and salt. Work butter into dry ingredients by hand until mixture resembles fine bread crumbs. Beat egg with buttermilk in separate bowl. Gradually pour egg mixture into flour. Mix by hand. Dough will be very stiff. Turn onto floured board; knead several times. Shape into oval. Place in prepared pan. Cut an X in top with sharp knife. Bake 40–45 minutes. Remove from oven and brush top with melted butter. If desired, serve with Cucumber Dip. MAKES 1 LOAF.

Cucumber Dip

---

4 cups plain yogurt
1 medium cucumber, peeled, grated
1–3 cloves garlic, minced
2 tablespoons olive oil
1 teaspoon dried dill weed
salt and pepper to taste

Use fine mesh strainers to strain excess liquid from yogurt and cucumber. Place in bowl; add garlic, olive oil, dill weed, salt, and pepper. Mix well. Serve as dip for whole wheat bread or vegetables. Makes approximately 4 cups.

Irish Soda Bread

3 cups all-purpose flour
⅔ cup sugar
1 tablespoon baking powder
1 teaspoon baking soda
1 teaspoon salt
½ cup raisins
2 eggs
1¾ cups buttermilk
2 tablespoons melted shortening

Preheat oven to 350 degrees. Grease a 5×9-inch loaf pan. Mix flour, sugar, baking powder, baking soda, and salt together in a large bowl. Add raisins. Mix eggs, buttermilk, and shortening; stir into flour. Pour into prepared pan. Bake for 60 minutes or until loaf is beginning to brown around the edges and the center springs back to the touch. Serve with Apple Butter (page 142). Makes 1 loaf.

Apple Butter

10 cups peeled, cored, chopped apples
1½ cups water
2½ cups sugar
½ cup apple juice
¼ teaspoon cinnamon
⅛ teaspoon ground cloves

Boil apples in water until soft. Blend apples and water in food processor or blender. Add sugar, apple juice, cinnamon, and cloves. Place in slow cooker and cook for 6 hours or until thickened to desired consistency. Serve on Irish Soda Bread (page 141). MAKES APPROXIMATELY 1 QUART.

She [Celia Robinson O'Dell] was a fun-loving grandmother who had lived in a Florida retirement complex but decided she preferred snowball fights to shuffleboard. She cooked, did volunteer work, and made everyone happy with her merry laughter. (**Brought Down the House**)

Mr. O'Dell had been a school janitor for forty years and had shepherded thousands of students through adolescence—answering their questions, solving their problems, and lending them lunch money. "Janitor" was a revered title in Pickax, and if Mr. O'Dell ever decided to run for the office of mayor, he would be elected unanimously. Now with his silver hair and ruddy complexion and benign expression . . . (**Knew Shakespeare**)

Salads and Side Dishes

Creamy Orange Delight

2 3-ounce packages orange gelatin
2 cups boiling water
1 6-ounce container orange juice concentrate, thawed
1 pint whipping cream, whipped
2 tablespoons powdered sugar
½ teaspoon vanilla extract
2 11-ounce cans mandarin oranges

Dissolve gelatin in boiling water. Add orange juice concentrate; stir well. Chill until partially set. With mixer, beat whipping cream until stiff peaks form. Fold in sugar and vanilla. Add whipping cream and oranges to gelatin. Beat until well blended. Chill until set. SERVES 8.

Cabbage-Beet Slaw

2 cups sliced potatoes
1½ cups frozen peas
6 cups shredded cabbage
1½ cups sliced cucumbers
1½ cups fresh or canned beets, drained
1½ cups cooked ham, finely diced
¾ cup olive oil
¼ cup cider vinegar
1 clove garlic
¾ teaspoon salt
¼ teaspoon pepper
1 cup sour cream

Boil potatoes in salted water until tender; drain and cool. Cook peas according to package directions; drain and cool. Place cabbage, cucumbers, beets, ham, potatoes, and peas in a large bowl. Blend oil, vinegar, garlic, salt, and pepper in blender. Pour over vegetables and ham. Refrigerate 50–60 minutes. Add sour cream and toss gently before serving. SERVES 12.

Baked Parsnips

2–2½ pounds parsnips
1 14-ounce can beef broth
3 tablespoons butter
½ teaspoon salt
¼ teaspoon pepper
¼ teaspoon nutmeg

*P*reheat oven to 350 degrees. Peel and quarter parsnips; parboil 15 minutes. In a separate pan, bring broth, butter, salt, pepper, and nutmeg to a boil. Place parsnips in large baking dish; add broth mixture. Bake 25 minutes. SERVES 4–6.

Creamed Kale

½ cup minced onion
4 tablespoons butter
½ cup chicken broth
½ cup half-and-half
dash nutmeg
salt and pepper
4 cups chopped, cooked kale

*I*n saucepan, sauté onion in butter until onion is soft. Add broth, half-and-half, nutmeg, salt, and pepper to taste. Cook until slightly reduced. Stir kale into broth mixture. SERVES 8.

Onion Relish

4 cups ground sweet onions
1 tablespoon salt
¾ cup vinegar
¼ teaspoon turmeric
½ teaspoon whole mixed pickling spice
⅔ cup sugar

Place onions and salt in small bowl. Let stand 30 minutes. Strain excess juice; do not rinse. Place onions and rest of ingredients in large saucepan. Boil 15 minutes; stirring often. Chill. MAKES APPROXIMATELY 1 QUART.

Polly said, "There's nothing to equal the flavor of Moose County Potatoes!"

"We all know why," said Arch. "A potato farmer was using them to make hard liquor during Prohibition, and the revenue agents caught him and poured it all on the ground . . . pass the potatoes, Millie."

She said, "Do you know why we have so many potato growers in Moose County? They came from Ireland during the Great Potato Famine in the nineteenth century. There was a blight on the crop, and a million Irish died of starvation, disease, or drowning when they tried to escape in leaky boats owned by unscrupulous profiteers . . . Sorry! Once a schoolteacher, always a schoolteacher." (**Dropped a Bombshell**)

Scalloped Potatoes

---

6 medium potatoes
2 tablespoons butter
2 tablespoons all-purpose flour
1½ cups milk
1 teaspoon salt
⅓ cup chopped onions

Preheat oven to 350 degrees. Peel and slice potatoes; place in a bowl of cold water and set aside. To make sauce, melt butter in small pan. Stir in flour; add milk and salt. Stir and cook until mixture begins to thicken. Remove from heat. Drain water from potatoes. Place half the potatoes in greased 2-quart baking dish. Place half the onions on potatoes. Pour half of the sauce over potatoes. Add remaining potatoes and onions. Pour remaining sauce over potatoes. Cover and bake 30 minutes. Uncover and bake 30 minutes more or until potatoes are fork-tender. SERVES 6.

Potato-Spinach Casserole

---

1 10-ounce package frozen, chopped spinach
4 large potatoes
¼ cup sour cream
¼ cup milk
1 teaspoon salt
3 tablespoons melted butter
2 tablespoons chopped onion
1 teaspoon dried dill weed

Cook spinach according to package directions, drain. Peel, slice, and boil potatoes, drain. Mash potatoes, adding sour cream, milk, salt, and 1 tablespoon melted butter. Saute onion in 1 tablespoon melted butter. Stir onion, dill weed, and spinach into potatoes. Drizzle 1 tablespoon melted butter over top. Bake in greased 1½ quart casserole 20 minutes. Serves 6–8.

Irish Boxty

---

1 large potato, pared
1 cup mashed potatoes
2 cups all-purpose flour
1 teaspoon baking powder
½ teaspoon salt
3 tablespoons butter, melted + butter for frying
¼ cup milk
oil

Grate potato and place in water to keep from discoloring. When ready to use, drain and squeeze potato with paper towels to remove excess liquid and place in a bowl. Stir in mashed potatoes. Mix flour, baking powder, and salt together. Stir into potato mixture. Add 3 tablespoons butter and milk to form a dough. Knead gently on floured surface. Divide into 16 patties. Fry in remaining butter and oil. SERVES 8.

The tiny Moose County potatoes, boiled in their skins, had an Irish flavor . . . (**Knew a Cardinal**)

Celia's Mustard Potato Salad

1 cup finely chopped celery
1 cup finely chopped onion
½ cup dill pickle relish, drained
1 cup mayonnaise
2 tablespoons prepared yellow mustard
2 teaspoons paprika
2 teaspoons celery seed
4 boiled eggs, chopped
10 cups diced, cooked potatoes

Thoroughly mix celery, onion, relish, mayonnaise, mustard, paprika, and celery seed in a large bowl. Fold in eggs. Pour over potatoes and gently mix. Chill. SERVES 4–6.

Meat

Wrap Platter

Corned Beef Wrap
4 8-inch flour tortillas
4 tablespoons mayonnaise
4 tablespoons sweet pickle relish
8 slices corned beef, thinly sliced
8 slices baby Swiss cheese, thinly sliced
2 cups grated cabbage

Spread lower half of each tortilla with 1 tablespoon mayonnaise. Sprinkle with 1 tablespoon relish. Top with 2 slices corned beef, 2 slices cheese, and ½ cup cabbage. Roll tortillas tightly, starting with lower half. Cut in halves or quarters.

Vegetarian Wrap
¼ cup garlic and herb spreadable cheese
¼ cup hummus
4 8-inch sun-dried tomato flour tortillas
8 slices Havarti cheese, thinly sliced
4 tablespoons chopped, seeded tomatoes
8 2×½-inch strips avocado
1 cup mixed sprouts
1 cup baby spinach leaves

Mix cheese spread and hummus. Spread 2 tablespoonfuls on the lower half of each tortilla. Top with 2 slices cheese, 1 tablespoon tomato, 2 strips avocado, ¼ cup sprouts, and ¼ cup spinach leaves. Roll tortillas tightly, starting with lower half. Cut in halves or quarters.

Club Wrap

¼ cup mayonnaise
4 8-inch flour tortillas
1 teaspoon dried basil leaves
4 slices turkey, thinly sliced
4 slices ham, thinly sliced
4 strips bacon, cooked, cooled
4 slices Muenster cheese, thinly sliced
4 tablespoons chopped, seeded tomatoes
1 cup shredded lettuce

Spread 1 tablespoon mayonnaise on lower half of each tortilla. Sprinkle ¼ teaspoon basil on mayonnaise. Top with 1 slice turkey, 1 slice ham, 1 strip bacon, 1 slice cheese, 1 tablespoon tomato, and ¼ cup lettuce. Roll tortillas tightly, starting with lower half. Cut in halves or quarters.

"How do you like living on Pleasant Street?" Qwilleran asked Celia.

"Oh, it's a wonderful big house I'm going to need now that I'm going into the catering business seriously. But I enjoyed living in the carriage house and running over with goodies for you and the kitties. I can still cook a few things for your freezer, you know, and Pat can deliver them when he does your yard work."

"That'll be much appreciated by all three of us." (**Robbed a Bank**)

Shepherd's Pie

---

2 tablespoons butter
½ cup chopped onion
1 clove garlic, minced
1 cup thinly sliced carrots
4 tablespoons all-purpose flour
2 cups beef broth (1 14-ounce can beef broth + water to make 2 cups)
1 teaspoon dried parsley
½ teaspoon dried thyme
½ teaspoon salt
½ teaspoon pepper
1 pound cooked, minced lamb or beef
4 cups mashed potatoes
½ cup shredded Irish Cheddar cheese, or mild Cheddar cheese

Preheat oven to 350 degrees. Melt butter in large skillet. Add onion, garlic, and carrots. Cook over low heat until onions are tender. Add flour; stir until well blended. Slowly add the broth, parsley, thyme, salt, and pepper, cooking until slightly thickened. Add meat and bring to a boil. Place in a casserole dish. Cover with mashed potatoes. Bake for 20 minutes; top with cheese and bake for an additional 10 minutes. Serves 6.

Stuffed Chicken

1 4-ounce block Irish Cheddar cheese
4 boneless, skinless chicken breasts, slightly frozen
¾ cup commercially prepared toasted bread crumbs
1 teaspoon dried basil leaves
1 teaspoon ground thyme
½ teaspoon salt
2 eggs, beaten

*P*reheat oven to 350 degrees. Cut 4 slices cheese from block, approximately 1×3×¼-inch in size. Insert sharp knife into side of each chicken breast and cut a pocket large enough for the slices of cheese. (Chicken is easier to cut into if slightly frozen.) Insert 1 slice cheese in each pocket. Grate the rest of the cheese. Mix bread crumbs, grated cheese, basil, thyme, and salt. Dip chicken in egg and then roll firmly in bread crumb mixture. Place in baking dish and bake uncovered approximately 30 minutes or until juices run clear. SERVES 4.

"We're so busy! I had to hire a helper. We're catering a wedding reception Saturday." [said Celia]
"Will you have time left for volunteer work? You were a real asset." [said Qwilleran]
"Only one thing—teaching adults to read. My first student is a forty-year-old woman who's tickled to be able to read recipe books." (**Robbed a Bank**)

Pat's Dublin Coddle

½ pound bacon slices
1 pound smoked sausages
½ cup all-purpose flour
1 teaspoon + 1 teaspoon dried parsley
½ teaspoon salt
½ teaspoon pepper
4 medium potatoes, peeled and cut into thick slices
2 medium carrots, peeled and cut into thick slices
1 clove garlic, minced
1 cup beef broth

Cut bacon slices into quarters; fry in skillet until soft and partially cooked. Remove bacon and place in stockpot. Slice sausages into large pieces. Mix together flour, 1 teaspoon parsley, salt, and pepper. Dip pieces of sausage into flour mixture. Fry in bacon grease. Remove to stockpot. Add potatoes, carrots, garlic, 1 teaspoon parsley, and broth. With large spoon, gently mix meats and vegetables. Cover and simmer on top of stove for 60 minutes. SERVES 6.

He [Qwilleran] liked to snoop in matters that were none of his business—propelled by curiosity or suspicion—and he had relied on Celia to preserve his anonymity. She was an ideal under-cover agent, being a respectable, trustworthy, grandmotherly type. And as an avid reader of spy fiction, she enjoyed being assigned to covert missions. There had been briefings, cryptic phone calls, hidden tape recorders, and secret meetings in the produce department at Toodle's Market. Now, as a married woman, how long could she retain her cover? (**Robbed a Bank**)

Whiskey-Baked Ham

1 5–7-pound semiboneless half ham
1 onion, quartered
2 bay leaves
4 cloves
4 peppercorns
2 tablespoons + ½ cup brown sugar, firmly packed
2 tablespoons vinegar
½ cup Irish whiskey
2 tablespoons spicy brown mustard

Place ham in large stockpot and cover with water. Add onion, bay leaves, cloves, peppercorns, 2 tablespoons sugar, and vinegar. Slowly bring to a boil. Reduce heat and simmer 15 minutes. Remove from water. Preheat oven to 325 degrees. Remove the rind from the ham. Brush ham with whiskey, reserving 2 tablespoonfuls. Place ham in oven. Bake 25 minutes per pound, or until internal temperature reaches 160 degrees. Mix the remaining 2 tablespoons whiskey with ½ cup brown sugar and mustard to make glaze. During last 15 minutes of baking, glaze ham several times. Slice thinly. SERVES 8–10.

Dilled Fish

½ cup sour cream
1 tablespoon all-purpose flour
1 tablespoon finely chopped onion
2 tablespoons milk
1 tablespoon dried parsley flakes
1 teaspoon dried dill weed
salt and pepper to taste
1½ pounds fresh fish fillets such as orange roughy or flounder.

Preheat oven to 350 degrees. Grease a shallow casserole dish. Mix sour cream, flour, onion, milk, parsley, dill weed, salt, and pepper together to make sauce. Place fish in prepared casserole dish. Pour sauce over fish. Cover and bake 20–25 minutes or until fish flakes easily with fork. SERVES 4.

It was after eleven, but he [Qwilleran] knew she [Celia] would be awake, reading spy fiction or baking cookies or talking to her grandson Down Below at late-night rates. Celia Robinson had found her way to Pickax through her acquaintance with the late Euphonia Gage, and she had found her way into local hearts with her volunteer work and cheerful disposition. Although Celia had the gray hair of age, she had the laughter of youth. (**Sang for the Birds**)

Desserts

Potookies
(Potato Chip Cookies)

2 cups butter, softened
1 cup sugar
2 teaspoons vanilla extract
3½ cups all-purpose flour
2 cups finely crushed potato chips
2 cups powdered sugar

Cream butter and sugar. Add vanilla. Mix in flour and potato chips. Drop by rounded teaspoonfuls onto ungreased cookie sheet. Bake 10–12 minutes. Dust with powdered sugar. Makes 6 dozen.

Erin's Barley Pudding

2 cups cooked pearl barley
4 cups diced apples
1 cup apple juice
2 tablespoons lemon juice
1 cup heavy cream

Follow package directions to cook barley. In medium saucepan, simmer cooked barley, apples, apple juice, and lemon juice until apples are tender and liquid is slightly reduced. Remove from heat. Use a hand blender or food processor to puree the pudding. Return to heat and bring to a boil. Chill. To serve, pour cream over top. SERVES 8.

The Uglies

1 8-ounce package cream cheese
1 egg
⅓ cup + 1 cup sugar
1 cup mini semisweet chocolate chips
1½ cups all-purpose flour
¼ cup cocoa
1 teaspoon baking soda
¼ teaspoon salt
1 cup water
½ cup oil
1 tablespoon vinegar
½ teaspoon vanilla extract
sliced almonds

Preheat oven to 350 degrees. Mix cream cheese, egg, and ⅓ cup sugar together; stir in chocolate chips. Set aside. Mix flour, 1 cup sugar, cocoa, baking soda, and salt together. Stir in water, oil, vinegar, and vanilla. Beat well. Fill paper-lined cupcake pans ⅓ full of batter. Top each with 1 heaping teaspoonful of cream cheese mixture. Add a few sliced almonds to top of cream cheese. Bake 25–30 minutes. MAKES 18–24 MEDIUM CUPCAKES.

Moose County Candy Potatoes

5 cups powdered sugar
6 tablespoons butter, melted
¾ cup flaked coconut
¼ cup brown sugar, firmly packed
2 teaspoons cinnamon

Mix powdered sugar and butter until well-blended. Add coconut and continue mixing until the coconut is well distributed throughout. Mix brown sugar and cinnamon together in a quart-sized plastic bag. Shape tablespoonfuls of coconut mixture into ovals resembling potatoes. Immediately shake coconut "potatoes" in brown sugar mixture. Use rounded end of toothpick to press indentations to make "eyes" in potatoes. MAKES APPROXIMATELY 30 "POTATOES."

Lying there awake he [Qwilleran] remembered his houseman's prediction when he first saw the renovated barn. The white-haired and highly respected Pat O'Dell had been custodian of the Pickax high school before retiring and starting his own janitorial service. He gazed up at the lofty beams and said in a fearful voice, "Will yourself be livin' here?" (**Knew a Cardinal**)

Chocolate "Mousse County" Ice Cream

1 cup sugar
2 cups half-and-half
1 cup heavy cream
2 cups milk
3 egg yolks, beaten
4 1-ounce squares semisweet chocolate, melted
1 teaspoon vanilla extract

Combine sugar, half-and-half, cream, and milk in saucepan. Cook over medium heat until milk is scalded (150 degrees) and sugar is dissolved, stirring constantly. Do not boil. Whisk several tablespoonfuls of milk mixture into egg yolks. Return egg mixture to the milk and cook a few minutes until mixture thickens slightly. Strain mixture into a bowl and add melted chocolate and vanilla. Stir until well blended. Chill until cool. Pour mixture into ice cream maker and follow manufacturer's directions for freezing. SERVES 6.

Whiskey Cake

1⅓ cups sugar
⅔ cup butter, softened
4 eggs
2½ cups all-purpose flour
1 teaspoon baking powder
½ teaspoon salt
⅔ cup whiskey or apple juice
1½ cups chopped walnuts
⅔ cup raisins

Preheat oven to 350 degrees. Grease a tube pan. Cream sugar and butter. Add eggs, one at a time. Mix flour, baking powder, and salt together. Add to sugar mixture, alternating dry ingredients with whiskey or apple juice. Fold in walnuts and raisins. Pour batter into prepared tube pan. Bake for 40 minutes or until cake springs back when touched lightly. Allow cake to cool 10 minutes before turning from pan. Frost with Chocolate Frosting. SERVES 10–12.

Chocolate Frosting
1 cup semisweet chocolate chips
½ cup half-and-half

Melt chocolate chips and half-and-half over low heat and stir until smooth . Pour chocolate frosting over cooled cake. Chill to set chocolate.

Kid's Table

Celia Robinson had married Pat O'Dell and had moved into his big house on Pleasant Street, leaving the carriage-house apartment vacant. (**Robbed a Bank**)

"Celia! I've been trying to call you and extend felicitations on your marriage, but you're hard to reach." [said Qwilleran]
"We took a little honeymoon trip. We went to see Pat's married daughter in Green Bay. He has three grandchildren. (**Robbed a Bank**)

"Will yourself [Qwilleran] be needin' me tomorrow, now? It's a new grandson I have in Kennebeck, and the urge is upon me to lay eyes on the mite of a boy." [said Pat O'Dell]
"By all means take the day off, Mr. O'Dell," said Qwilleran. (**Sniffed Glue**)

Strawberry Lemonade

1¾ cups fresh lemon juice
1 3-ounce package strawberry gelatin
2 cups sugar
3 quarts water

In a gallon container, stir together lemon juice, gelatin, sugar, and water. Chill before serving. Makes approximately 1 gallon.

Carrotpillars

3 stalks celery
1 3-ounce package cream cheese
dash garlic powder
3 drops yellow food coloring
milk
2 small carrots
24 chow mein noodles

To make caterpillars (carrotpillars) cut each celery stalk into 4 equal pieces. In a small bowl, mix cream cheese, garlic powder, food coloring, and enough milk to thin cream cheese to spreading consistency. Fill celery stalks with cream cheese mixture. Thinly slice carrots and place 4 or 5 slices on top of cream cheese to resemble spots on the back of the celery "carrotpillars." Place two chow mein noodles on one end of the celery in the cream cheese to resemble antennae. Makes 12 "carrotpillars."

PB & J Surprise

2 8-ounce cans crescent dinner rolls
½ cup crunchy peanut butter
1 egg
⅓ cup sugar
1 tablespoon all-purpose flour
½ teaspoon baking powder
¼ cup concord grape jelly

Preheat oven to 350 degrees. Unroll one can of crescent dinner rolls on an ungreased cookie sheet. Pinch seams of dough together. In a small bowl, mix together peanut butter, egg, sugar, flour, and baking powder. Spread peanut butter mixture over crescent rolls. Open second can of rolls; unroll and pinch together seams. Spread jelly on dough. Beginning with the longer side, roll dough into a spiral. Using a sharp knife, cut spiral into 12 rounds. Arrange rounds on top of peanut butter mixture. Bake for 25 minutes. Remove from oven and cut into 12 pieces around the jelly rounds. SERVES 12.

Tiny Burgers

1 pound extra-lean ground beef
seasoned salt to taste
pepper to taste
4 slices cheese
8 small dinner rolls

Divide ground beef into 8 patties. Sprinkle with seasoned salt and pepper. Fry or grill patties. Divide cheese into halves. Place one half on each tiny burger. Put burgers in rolls. Serve with condiments such as relish, ketchup, mayonnaise, and mustard. MAKES 8 TINY BURGERS.

Lucky Rainbow

1 3-ounce package cherry gelatin
1 3-ounce package orange gelatin
1 3-ounce package lemon gelatin
1 3-ounce package lime gelatin
1 3-ounce package berry blue gelatin
1 3-ounce package grape gelatin
9 cups boiling water

In separate bowls, mix each package of gelatin with 1½ cups boiling water. Allow all to cool to room temperature except the cherry gelatin. Place the cherry gelatin in a 3-quart bowl, preferably clear glass. Refrigerate until set but not firm. Spoon orange gelatin over cherry gelatin. Let set until nearly congealed and add lemon gelatin. Repeat with lime, berry blue, and grape gelatins. Refrigerate until set. SERVES 8–10.

Golden Macaroni

2 cups elbow macaroni
1 15-ounce jar cheese dip
2 tablespoons butter
¼ teaspoon dry mustard
¼ teaspoon paprika
½ teaspoon salt
¼ cup sour cream

Cook macaroni according to package directions; drain. While macaroni is cooking, melt cheese in microwave oven or in saucepan over low heat. Add butter, mustard, paprika, and salt. Stir until mixed thoroughly. Remove from heat. Stir into macaroni. Fold in sour cream. SERVES 6–8.

Celia would be forever young. She and Pat still had snowball fights, according to their amused neighbors. (**Brought Down the House**)

Celia's Summer Snowballs

1 cup sugar
3 cups miniature marshmallows
water

Place sugar on plate. Place 1½ cups marshmallows in a bowl. Sprinkle with water. Scoop out by tablespoonfuls (approximately 7 marshmallows at a time) and gently press together; roll in sugar. Repeat with remaining marshmallows. Place on wax paper and allow to air dry. Fun as a treat in summer, nice in winter as a garnish for hot chocolate. MAKES APPROXIMATELY 36 SNOWBALLS.

Irish Oatmeal Cookies

½ cup butter
½ cup shortening
1 cup sugar
1 cup brown sugar, firmly packed
2 eggs
1 teaspoon vanilla extract
¾ cup whole wheat flour
¾ cup all-purpose flour
1 teaspoon baking powder
½ teaspoon baking soda
½ teaspoon salt
1 cup chopped walnuts
3 cups quick-cooking Irish oatmeal

Preheat oven to 350 degrees. Cream together butter, shortening, and sugars. Add eggs and vanilla, blending well. In small bowl, mix flours, baking powder, baking soda, and salt. Add to creamed ingredients. Fold in walnuts and oatmeal. Drop by rounded tablespoonfuls onto ungreased cookie sheet. Bake 10–12 minutes or until done. Take from oven and wait 3 minutes before removing to cooling rack. MAKES 4 DOZEN.

"How old are you Celia? [asked Qwilleran] I don't usually ask women their age, but this is important."
   "Seventy," she said shyly.
   "Then you've paid your dues. You've raised a family and worked on a farm for half a century. You're healthy. You have long years ahead of you. It's your turn to live your own life."
(Sang for the Birds)

Lanspeak
Reunion

Please join us in West Middle Hummock for a family reunion on June 25 at 11:00. Bring your bathing suits and tennis rackets for an afternoon of fun and fellowship. Plan to stay through the evening for snacking and good times, when we continue our annual games tournament.

Carol and Larry

At first glance the Lanspeaks were a plain-looking middle-aged couple, but they had a youthful source of energy that made them civic leaders and genial company as well as excellent actors. Qwilleran often wondered what they ate for breakfast. (**Knew a Cardinal**)

Beverages and Breads

Mimosa

3 ounces orange juice
3 ounces champagne
2–3 ice cubes

Place ice in collins glass. Pour chilled orange juice over ice. Add champagne. Stir gently.

Vanilla-Bean Coffee

1 vanilla bean
2⅔ cups milk
3 tablespoons brown sugar
6 cups brewed coffee

Slice and scrape out vanilla bean and place in a pan with milk and brown sugar. Bring mixture to a boil, stirring occasionally. Remove the vanilla bean. Add milk mixture to coffee. SERVES 8.

Oatmeal Muffins

Topping
⅔ cup brown sugar, firmly packed
2 tablespoons all-purpose flour
2 tablespoons melted butter

Preheat oven to 425 degrees. Grease muffin pan; set aside. To make topping, mix brown sugar, flour, and melted butter until crumbly.

Muffins
1 cup all-purpose flour
¼ cup sugar
3 teaspoons baking powder
½ teaspoon salt
3 tablespoons shortening
1 cup uncooked rolled oats
1 egg
1 cup milk

Mix flour, sugar, baking powder, and salt. Cut shortening into flour mixture. Blend in the oats. Gently stir in egg and milk. Fill greased muffin pans ⅔ full. Sprinkle with topping. Bake 15–20 minutes. MAKES 18 MUFFINS.

Biscuit Trio

Chocolate Biscuits
2 cups all-purpose flour
1 tablespoon baking powder
½ teaspoon salt
2 tablespoons sugar
½ cup shortening
⅔ cup milk
1 1-ounce square chocolate, melted
1 tablespoon melted butter

Preheat oven to 450 degrees. Mix flour, baking powder, salt, and sugar. Cut shortening into flour mixture until mixture is crumbly. Add milk all at once; blend well. Stir in chocolate. Dough will be sticky. Place on generously floured surface. Sprinkle with additional flour. Pat out to ½-inch thickness. Cut with a 1½-inch biscuit cutter. Place on ungreased cookie sheet. Brush tops with melted butter. Bake 10–12 minutes. Serve with Chocolate Butter. MAKES APPROXIMATELY 3 DOZEN BISCUITS.

Chocolate Butter
4 teaspoons cocoa
4 teaspoons powdered sugar
½ cup butter, softened

Stir cocoa and sugar into butter; mix well. Serve with Chocolate Biscuits.

Herbed Biscuits

2 cups all-purpose flour
1 tablespoon baking powder
½ teaspoon salt
⅓ cup shortening
2 tablespoons butter
⅔ cup milk
1 teaspoon dried dill weed
½ teaspoon dried tarragon

Preheat oven to 425 degrees. Mix flour, baking powder, and salt. Cut shortening and butter into flour mixture until mixture is crumbly. Add milk all at once; blend well. Stir in dill weed and tarragon. Dough will be soft. Place on floured surface. Sprinkle top with additional flour. Pat out to ½-inch thickness. Cut with 1½-inch biscuit cutter. Place on ungreased cookie sheet. Bake 10–12 minutes. Serve with Basil Butter. MAKES APPROXIMATELY 3 DOZEN BISCUITS.

Basil Butter

2 teaspoons dried basil
½ cup butter, softened

Mix basil and butter thoroughly. Let stand 30 minutes so that basil flavor will be infused into the butter. Serve with Herbed Biscuits.

Sour Cream Biscuits
1 tablespoon baking powder
½ cup butter
1 cup sour cream

Preheat oven to 425 degrees. Mix flour and baking powder. Cut butter into flour mixture until mixture is crumbly. Add sour cream and stir until mixed well. Dough will be soft. Place on floured surface. Sprinkle top with additional flour. Pat out to ½-inch thickness. Cut with 1½-inch biscuit cutter. Bake 10–12 minutes. Serve with Ginger Butter. MAKES APPROXIMATELY 3 DOZEN BISCUITS.

Ginger Butter
¼ cup light corn syrup
½ teaspoon ground ginger
½ cup butter, softened

Stir corn syrup and ginger into butter; mix well. Serve with Sour Cream Biscuits.

Larry Lanspeak was president of the Historical Society and chairperson of the Goodwinter Farmhouse Museum, as well as owner of the local department store. As merchant, civic leader, and talented actor in the Pickax Theater Club, he brought boundless energy to everything he undertook. Qwilleran put in a call to the Lanspeak country house in fashionable West Middle Hummock, and, although it was almost two o'clock, Larry answered the phone as briskly as he would in midday. (**Talked to Ghosts**)

Larry's Coffee Cake

2 cups brown sugar, firmly packed
2 cups all-purpose flour
¾ cup shortening
½ cup chopped walnuts
1 egg
1 teaspoon vanilla extract
1 cup hot coffee
1 teaspoon baking soda

Preheat oven to 350 degrees. Grease and flour a 9×13-inch baking pan. Mix sugar, flour, and shortening until crumbly. Stir nuts into 1 cup of sugar mixture and reserve for topping. Add egg and vanilla to remaining sugar mixture. Mix hot coffee and baking soda in small bowl and add to sugar mixture. Mixture will be very thin. Pour into prepared baking pan. Top with reserved nut mixture. Bake 25–30 minutes. SERVES 8–10.

Qwilleran said, "Carol, you're so well organized, it's unnerving."

"Well, it helps if you've run a department store for twenty-five years . . . and directed two dozen stage productions . . . and raised three kids." (**Robbed a Bank**)

Brunch Nut Spiral

¾ cup milk
1 package yeast
¼ cup warm water
¼ cup + ½ cup sugar
1 teaspoon salt
¼ cup shortening
3–3½ cups all-purpose flour
6 tablespoons soft butter
¼ cup brown sugar, firmly packed
1 cup finely chopped walnuts
1 cup finely chopped pecans
oil

Scald milk (150 degrees); cool to lukewarm (110 degrees). Put yeast in warm water in bottom of large bowl. After yeast dissolves, add ¼ cup sugar, salt, shortening, milk, and enough flour to make soft dough. Knead on lightly floured surface, folding dough over and giving a quarter turn each time, until smooth and elastic. Place in greased bowl, turning over once to coat all sides. Cover with cloth; let rise 1½–2 hours until double in size. Punch down. Shape into ball; roll out into 16×20-inch rectangle. Mix butter, ½ cup sugar, brown sugar, and nuts until crumbly. Spread nut mixture on dough. Roll dough as for jelly roll starting with 16-inch side. Place on greased cookie sheet diagonally, seam side down. Brush top with a little oil. Cover with towel. Let rise 45 minutes. During last 10 minutes of rise, preheat oven to 350 degrees. Bake 40–45 minutes. Cool; slice thin. MAKES 16 1-INCH SLICES.

The two men walked to their cars and drove up Black Creek Lane, Larry in the long station wagon that signified a moneyed country estate, and Qwilleran in his economy-model compact. (**Talked to Ghosts**)

"Don't kid yourself, Qwill. [said Mildred] There's plenty of old money up here. They don't flaunt it, but they've got it—people like Doctor Zoller, Euphonia Gage, Doctor Halifax, the Lanspeaks, and how about you?" (**Talked to Ghosts**)

Qwilleran punched the number of the Lanspeak residence, visualizing their attractive country house as he waited for them to answer: split-rail fences, cedar shake roof, picturesque barn. (**Sniffed Glue**)

Side Dishes

Larry, looking immaculate in his custom-tailored suit and highly polished wingtips, said, "Don't let me stay more than twenty minutes. I'm ushering today." The Lanspeaks attended the Old Stone Church across the park from the Klingenschoen Theatre—the largest, oldest, wealthiest congregation in town. (**Knew a Cardinal**)

Carol's Sunshine Fruit Terrine

½ cup sugar
1¼ cups water
2 envelopes unflavored gelatin

1 24-ounce jar citrus salad (grapefruits and oranges), drained
1 24½-ounce jar tropical fruit (pineapple and papaya), drained
1 15-ounce can mandarin oranges, drained

Spray a loaf pan with cooking spray. Line pan with plastic wrap. Place sugar and water in small saucepan. Sprinkle gelatin over water and allow it to soften, about 3 minutes. Cook over low heat until gelatin and sugar are completely dissolved. Remove from heat and cool but do not chill. Arrange fruit in layers, keeping the same type of fruit in the same rows in the loaf pan. Pour cooled gelatin mixture over fruit. Lay a piece of plastic wrap on the top of the terrine. Chill overnight. To serve, remove plastic wrap from top of terrine. Place a platter over the terrine and invert. Remove pan and plastic wrap. Slice terrine with serrated knife. SERVES 8.

"You know very well that Larry would love to fly you down to Chicago or Minneapolis. He's bought a new four-seater. Polly and I could go along for a shopping binge. Or maybe she'd like to see the game, too." [said Carol] (**Knew a Cardinal**)

Ambrosia

5 navel oranges
1 6-ounce jar maraschino cherries
1 cup shredded canned coconut
1 16-ounce can crushed pineapple, drained
2 tablespoons powdered sugar

Pare and cut oranges into bite-sized pieces. Rinse and cut cherries into halves. Place in medium-sized bowl. Add the coconut, pineapple, and powdered sugar to the oranges and cherries. Stir and chill. SERVES 10–12.

Cheesy Grits

4 cups water
¼ teaspoon salt
1 cup quick grits
⅓ cup heavy cream
1 cup shredded Cheddar cheese
2 tablespoons butter
Prepared sliced jalapeño peppers to taste

Bring water and salt to a boil. Stir in grits. Reduce heat to medium. Cook 5 minutes, stirring occasionally, or until thickened. Stir in cream, cheese, butter, and jalapeño pepper, if using. SERVES 4–6.

At six o'clock Qwilleran picked up Polly in Indian Village for the drive to West Middle Hummock, where the Lanspeaks had their country estate . . . The Lanspeaks lived in an unpretentious farmhouse furnished with country antiques that looked like museum quality. When their children were young, they had kept a family cow, riding horses, and a few chickens and ducks. Now Carol and Larry were alone—except for the couple who took care of the housekeeping and grounds—and they concentrated on running the department store and participating in the theater club, historical society, genealogy club, and gourmet group. (**Robbed a Bank**)

Fried Green Tomatoes

4 green tomatoes
salt and pepper to taste
½ cup yellow cornmeal
½ cup all-purpose flour
dash of celery salt
oil

Cut tomatoes into ¼–½-inch slices. Sprinkle one side with salt and pepper. Mix cornmeal, flour, and celery salt. Coat both sides of tomatoes with cornmeal mixture. Fry in hot oil about 3 minutes each side or until golden brown. Serve with Horseradish Sauce. Serves 6–8.

Horseradish Sauce

4 ounces cream cheese, room temperature
¾ cup sour cream
¾ cup milk
4 teaspoons prepared horseradish or to taste

Place cream cheese, sour cream, and milk in a bowl and whip together. Fold in horseradish. Serve with Fried Green Tomatoes.

Despite the man's [Larry's] elevated standing in the community, he was unprepossessing. Ordinary height, ordinary coloring, and ordinary features gave him an anonymity that enabled him to slip into many different roles for the Theater Club. (**Talked to Ghosts**)

Creamy French Toast

---

1 3-ounce package cream cheese, room temperature
1 tablespoon + 2 tablespoons cream
1 teaspoon sugar
8 slices bread, about 1 inch thick
1 cup milk
½ teaspoon vanilla extract
3 eggs
2 tablespoons butter
3 tablespoons oil
Strawberry Syrup
fresh sliced strawberries

Mix cream cheese, 1 tablespoon cream, and sugar. Spread cream cheese mixture on 4 slices of bread. Top with the remaining slices. Whisk together milk, 2 tablespoons cream, vanilla, and eggs. Dip bread into the milk mixture, coating both sides. Heat the butter and oil in a large skillet or griddle and fry bread until brown on both sides. Top with Strawberry Syrup and strawberries. SERVES 4.

Strawberry Syrup

1 10-ounce package strawberries in syrup
¼ cup sugar
½ cup light corn syrup

Thaw strawberries in package. Do not drain. Place berries with liquid in food processor or use hand blender and process until smooth. Strain through a fine sieve. Place in saucepan with sugar and corn syrup. Bring to a boil over medium heat. Reduce heat and let simmer for 10 minutes. Skim off foam. Serve hot over French toast. MAKES 1½ CUPS.

180   **LANSPEAK REUNION**

What the Lanspeaks called their cottage [at Purple Point] had a tallcase clock in the foyer, a baby grand piano in the living room, a quadraphonic sound system, and four bedrooms on the balcony. The only reminder of the original fish camp was the cobblestone fireplace. (**Went into the Closet**)

Dr. Diane's Fruit-and-Nut Granola

½ cup butter
½ cup light corn syrup
1 cup chopped walnuts
1 cup chopped pecans
1 cup chopped cashews
1 cup slivered almonds
4–5 cups quick-cooking rolled oats
1½ cups raisins

Preheat oven to 350 degrees. Lightly grease 2 9×13-inch pans. Melt butter; add corn syrup and mix well. Pour into large bowl. Add nuts, then rolled oats. Mix well. Bake in prepared pans, stirring every 10 minutes until oats are golden brown. Add raisins for last 5 minutes or after mix is taken from oven. Store in airtight container. Serve over yogurt. MAKES APPROXIMATELY 10 CUPS.

Raspberry-Cream Cups

1 11-ounce package white baking chips
18 paper baking cups
1 10-ounce package frozen raspberries, thawed
1 10-ounce package marshmallows
1 8-ounce can crushed pineapple, drained
½ pint whipping cream
½ pint fresh raspberries

Melt baking chips according to package directions. Use the back of a spoon to spread a thin layer of the melted chocolate on the bottom and sides of the baking cups. Place in the refrigerator to set. Strain the raspberries to remove the seeds and place juice and pulp in a saucepan with marshmallows and pineapple. Cook and stir over low heat until marshmallows are melted. Let cool for 30 minutes. Beat whipping cream until stiff peaks form. Fold whipped cream into raspberry mixture. Spoon the raspberry cream into the white chocolate cups. Chill 2 hours or until set. Remove the paper baking cups. If any of the chocolate breaks away from the filling when removing the paper cups, press it back into the filling. Place fresh raspberries on top before serving. MAKES 18 CUPS.

The auditorium was a steeply raked amphitheatre with a thrust stage, and there was a gracious lobby. When Qwilleran arrived there Wednesday night, he found Larry Lanspeak in the lobby, bent over the drinking fountain.

"Your beard looks promising," he told the actor.

Larry rubbed his chin. "In two more weeks it should be good enough for an eleventh-century Scottish king." (**Wasn't There**)

. . . "Larry's a joy to direct, let me say that. [Dwight said] Now I know why he has such a great reputation in community theatre. I'd heard about him in Iowa before I knew there was any such place as Pickax." (**Wasn't There**)

Meats

Meat-and-Cheese Frittata

4 slices bacon
¼ pound ground sausage
⅓ cup diced ham
6 eggs
1 tablespoon oil
¾ cup shredded Cheddar cheese

Fry bacon, crumbled sausage, and ham separately. Drain on paper towels. Break bacon into large pieces. Beat eggs. Wipe out skillet and heat oil in it. Pour in eggs and top with meat and cheese. Cook, covered, over medium-low heat for 5 minutes or until eggs are set on the bottom, but still wet on the top. Place under broiler 2–3 minutes or until top is set. SERVES 4.

Asparagus and Bacon Quiche

2 cups bite-sized asparagus pieces (about 8 ounces)
1 ready-to-bake pie crust from 15-ounce package
4–6 thin slices baby Swiss cheese
5 eggs
½ cup milk
¼ cup fresh shredded Parmesan cheese
1 teaspoon dried basil leaves
½ teaspoon dried tarragon leaves
⅛ teaspoon salt
1 medium tomato, peeled, thinly sliced

Preheat oven to 350 degrees. Wash asparagus. Place into boiling water; boil 5 minutes or until tender-crisp. Plunge into ice water, drain, and set aside. Place crust in 9-inch pie pan. Arrange cheese slices over crust. Beat eggs and milk. Stir in Parmesan cheese, basil, tarragon, and salt. Pour egg mixture over Swiss cheese. Place asparagus on egg mixture. Top with tomato slices. Bake 30–35 minutes or until knife inserted in center comes out clean. Let stand 10 minutes before cutting. SERVES 6.

"Everything is very formal. Women have to wear hats to his Tuesday afternoon tea, and we've sold out of millinery. [said Carol Lanspeak] We sell the basic felt that women wear to church, but our daughter said we should gussy them up with feathers and flowers and huge ribbon bows. So we did! Diane is a sober, dedicated M.D., but she had a mad streak."
"Takes after her mother," Larry said. (**Robbed a Bank**)

Elegant Chicken Crepes

¼ cup chopped onion
4 tablespoons + 1 tablespoon melted butter
4 tablespoons + 1 cup all-purpose flour
1 14-ounce can chicken broth
½ teaspoon dried dill weed
1 cup diced cooked chicken
¼ cup grated fresh Parmesan cheese
½ cup canned or frozen cooked spinach, drained
¼ cup canned mushrooms, drained
1 egg, beaten
2 cups milk
¼ cup sliced almonds

Preheat oven to 350 degrees. Grease a casserole dish. Saute onion in 4 tablespoons butter. Stir in 4 tablespoons flour. Add broth and stir until mixture is thickened. Stir dill weed, chicken, cheese, spinach, and mushrooms into the sauce. Reserve 1 cup of sauce. To make crepes, mix egg, 1 tablespoon melted butter, milk, and 1 cup flour. Drop 2 tablespoonfuls of batter on lightly greased skillet. Tilt skillet to form round crepe. Cook crepe on one side only. Place heaping tablespoonful of filling on unbrowned side of crepe and roll. Place rolled crepe in prepared casserole dish. Repeat with remaining batter and sauce to make total of 12 crepes. Pour reserved 1 cup sauce over crepes and top with almonds. Bake for 15 minutes covered; uncover and bake 10 minutes more. SERVES 6.

Qwilleran crossed the street to the department store, his newshound instincts scenting a good story with human interest and a touch of humor. Lanspeaks was a large fourth-generation store with new-fashioned merchandise but old-fashioned ideas about customer service.
(Robbed a Bank)

Desserts

Cream Puffs

1 cup butter
2 cups water
2 cups all-purpose flour
8 eggs, room temperature

Preheat oven to 400 degrees. Lightly grease a cookie sheet. Bring butter and water to a boil in small saucepan. Reduce heat. Add flour all at once. Stir constantly over low heat until mixture forms a ball, approximately 1 minute. Remove from heat for 1 minute. Then add eggs one at a time, beating thoroughly after each egg until dough does not look slippery. Place on prepared cookie sheet by heaping tablespoonfuls, about 3 inches apart. Bake for 30–35 minutes. Cool. Cut tops off about ¼ way down. Remove soft dough from inside. MAKES ABOUT 6 DOZEN 2 TO 2½-INCH PUFFS.

Puff Filling
1 3-ounce cook-and-serve vanilla or chocolate pudding mix
½ pint whipping cream

Prepare pudding according to package directions. Cool. Whip cream until firm peaks form. Fold whipped cream into cooled pudding. Place a heaping tablespoonful into each puff and re-place top.

Chocolate Sauce
1 cup semisweet chocolate chips
½ cup half-and-half
½ teaspoon vanilla extract
1 teaspoon butter

Melt chocolate chips in double boiler. Stir in whipping cream slowly. Add vanilla and butter. Swirl by tablespoonful onto top of filled cream puffs. Chill cream puffs to set chocolate.

Chocolate Crown Meringue

4 egg whites
1 cup powdered sugar
2 tablespoons cocoa
½ teaspoon vanilla extract
1 teaspoon white vinegar
½ pint whipping cream
1 cup sliced strawberries
½ cup sliced almonds
chocolate syrup

Preheat oven to 250 degrees. Beat egg whites until stiff. Add sugar slowly while continuing to beat. Add cocoa, vanilla, and vinegar. Put foil on cookie sheet and pour egg white mixture on center, spreading into 9-inch circle. Form crown by building up outside edge of circle. Bake 60 minutes. Turn off heat and leave in oven 1 additional hour. Remove from oven and take from foil. Place on serving plate. Cool. Whip cream and spread on top. Arrange strawberries and almonds on top of whipped cream. Drizzle with chocolate syrup. Serves 6.

Evening Tournament Snacks

Crab Dip

1 cup sour cream
1 8-ounce package cream cheese, room temperature
2 tablespoons milk
1 tablespoon mayonnaise
1 teaspoon horseradish
3 tablespoons chili sauce
1 tablespoon fresh lemon juice
1 tablespoon finely chopped onion
2 6-ounce cans fancy white crabmeat, drained

Mix sour cream, cream cheese, and milk until smooth. Stir in mayonnaise, horseradish, chili sauce, lemon juice, and onion. Fold in crabmeat. If a thinner dip is desired, add more milk. Chill before serving. MAKES APPROXIMATELY 4 CUPS. Serve with toasted pita bread triangles, and/or vegetables such as cherry tomatoes, sugar peapods, carrots, and celery.

Marinated Beef Skewers with Dipping Sauce

3 pounds sirloin steak
½ cup soy sauce
½ cup water
2 tablespoons brown sugar, firmly packed
1 clove garlic, minced
1½ teaspoons grated gingerroot
skewers

Freeze meat for 1–1½ hours to make it easier to cut. Remove excess fat. Cut across grain into slices about ¼ inch thick. Combine soy sauce, water, brown sugar, garlic, and gingerroot. Marinate meat in soy sauce mixture about 1 hour. Remove from marinade and thread onto skewers. Discard marinade. Place on grill or broiler rack and cook 4 inches from heat for 7–9 minutes. Turn to brown other side. Serve with Dipping Sauce. SERVES 6–8.

Dipping Sauce
½ cup chili sauce
½ cup ketchup
⅓ cup molasses
⅔ cup orange juice
3 tablespoons finely chopped onion
2 tablespoons soy sauce
1 tablespoon Worcestershire sauce
2 tablespoons sugar
1 clove garlic, minced
¼ teaspoon ground ginger

Mix all ingredients together in saucepan. Bring to a boil over medium heat; reduce heat and simmer for 15 minutes. MAKES ABOUT 2 CUPS.

Peanut Butter Crunch Squares

1 cup extra crunchy peanut butter
½ cup sugar
½ cup light corn syrup
2¾ cups crushed cornflakes
1 12-ounce bag chocolate chips

Melt peanut butter, sugar, and corn syrup over medium heat, stirring constantly. Add cornflakes and mix well. Spread into 8×8-inch greased pan. Melt chocolate chips over low heat. Spread over top of cornflake mixture. Refrigerate to set chocolate. SERVES 8.

"How did your Macduff turn out?" [asked Qwilleran]
   "Better than I expected, especially in his scene with Macbeth. [said Dwight] When he has Larry to bounce off, he's really with it. Larry is a superb actor." (**Wasn't There**)

Dilled Chicken Spread

2 cups diced cooked chicken
½ cup mayonnaise
¼ cup plain yogurt
1½ teaspoons dried dill weed
salt and pepper to taste

Place all ingredients in mixing bowl and blend with electric mixer. Shape into a ball; chill. Serve with crackers. SERVES 6–8.

Pepper-Pear Sauce on Cream Cheese

6 hard pears
1 green pepper, seeded
1 small hot pepper, seeded
⅔ cup sugar
¼ cup cider vinegar
2 teaspoons salt
1 teaspoon celery seed
1 teaspoon mustard seed
1 8-ounce package cream cheese

Core pears but do not remove skins. Grind pears, green pepper, and hot pepper in a grinder or food processor. Place in medium saucepan. Add sugar, vinegar, salt, celery seed, and mustard seed. Bring to a boil over medium heat; reduce heat and simmer over low heat for 30 minutes. Chill. Place cream cheese in serving dish and pour pepper-pear sauce over top. Serve with crackers. SERVES 8–10.

The Lanspeaks amazed Qwilleran. Nothing in their appearance or manners suggested that they had been on the stage, yet Carol could play a queen or a harlot convincingly, and Larry could play the role of a scoundrel, old man, or dashing hero. Both had the inner energy that distinguished an outstanding performer. (**Robbed a Bank**)

Cardinal's Cracker Toffee

---

1 sleeve saltine crackers (36 crackers)
½ cup butter
½ cup brown sugar
1 cup semisweet chocolate chips
½ cup chopped pecans

Preheat oven to 400 degrees. Line a 10×15-inch jelly roll pan with aluminum foil. Arrange crackers in a single layer in pan. In small saucepan, melt butter with brown sugar. Boil over low heat for 3 minutes without stirring. Pour butter mixture over crackers. Bake for 5 minutes. Watch crackers the last minute to avoid scorching. Remove from oven and sprinkle chocolate chips over crackers. When chips melt, spread chocolate evenly over crackers. Sprinkle with nuts. Chill for 1 hour in the refrigerator. Remove from foil and break into pieces. SERVES 6–8.

Dale's Cinnamon Pecans

---

1 cup sugar
6 tablespoons evaporated milk
1½ teaspoons cinnamon
4 cups pecan halves

Butter a cookie sheet. Mix sugar, milk, and cinnamon in saucepan. Bring to a boil. Boil 2 minutes. Cool slightly. Place pecans in bowl. Pour sugar mixture over nuts. Stir nuts to coat on both sides. Transfer to prepared cookie sheet. Let nuts remain in small clusters or separate individually. Cool on sheet for several hours so coating can set. SERVES 8.

Cheese Ball

1 5-ounce jar sharp pasteurized process cheese spread
1 5-ounce jar process blue cheese spread
11 ounces cream cheese (1 8-ounce and 1 3-ounce package)
½ cup finely chopped celery
½ cup finely chopped onion
garlic powder to taste
chopped pecans

Thoroughly combine all ingredients except pecans. Shape into 1 large or 2 small balls. Roll mixture in chopped pecans. SERVES 8.

Salsa Pull-Apart Bread

4 7½-ounce cans buttermilk biscuits
5 tablespoons melted butter
1 cup salsa
1 cup grated Cheddar cheese

Preheat oven to 350 degrees. Grease a Bundt or tube pan. Cut biscuits into quarters. Dip biscuits into melted butter and put approximately 1½ cans of biscuits into prepared pan. Layer with half of the salsa and half of the cheese. Place approximately 1½ cans of biscuits on salsa and cheese; top with remaining salsa and cheese. Place remaining can of biscuits on top. Bake 35–40 minutes uncovered. Cool 10 minutes and invert on serving dish. Serve with Taco Dip. SERVES 10–12.

Taco Dip
1 cup sour cream
1–3 teaspoons taco seasoning

Mix sour cream and taco seasoning to taste. Dip biscuit sections into taco dip. Taco dip can be doubled if more dip is desired. Serves 8.

Carol and Larry Lanspeak, seated at a blue table, waved an invitation to Qwilleran and Polly to join them. Everyone liked the Lanspeaks, the affluent but down-to-earth owners of the department store. Both had given up acting careers in New York to carry on the family retailing tradition. Their talents were still put to good use in the theater club, and all other community projects received their generous support. (**Robbed a Bank**)

Cheese Wafers

1 cup butter, softened
16 ounces grated sharp Cheddar cheese, room temperature
½ teaspoon cayenne pepper or to taste
3 cups all-purpose flour

Preheat oven to 350 degrees. Lightly grease 2 cookie sheets. With a mixer combine butter, cheese, and pepper. Add flour and mix well to form dough. Shape into two logs about 2 inches in diameter. Cut into slices about ¼ inch in thickness. Place on prepared cookie sheets; press top of slices gently with fork tines. Bake 12–15 minutes. Remove from cookie sheets immediately and place on racks to cool. Makes 7 dozen.

Spinach Balls

2 10-ounce packages frozen chopped spinach
½ cup finely chopped onion
1 8-ounce can diced water chestnuts, drained, finely chopped
2½ cups commercially prepared herb-seasoned stuffing
½ cup fresh grated Parmesan cheese
4 eggs, beaten
¾ cup melted butter
½ teaspoon thyme
⅛ teaspoon garlic powder
¼ teaspoon salt
¼ teaspoon pepper

Cook spinach according to package directions; drain well. Place in mixing bowl. Stir in onion and water chestnuts. Add stuffing, cheese, eggs, and butter; mix to combine. Add thyme, garlic powder, salt, and pepper. Chill. Preheat oven to 350 degrees. Shape into walnut-sized balls. Bake 12–15 minutes or until lightly browned. MAKES APPROXIMATELY 4 DOZEN.

Caramel Crunch Popped Corn

1 cup butter
1 16-ounce box brown sugar
½ cup light corn syrup
1 teaspoon salt
½ teaspoon baking soda
1 teaspoon vanilla extract
28–30 cups popped popcorn

Preheat oven to 250 degrees. Line 2 9×13-inch pans with foil and grease. Melt butter in saucepan. Stir in sugar, corn syrup, and salt. Bring to a boil, stirring constantly. Boil 5 minutes without stirring. As soon as syrup mixture is removed from heat, stir in baking soda and vanilla. Put popped corn in prepared pans. Pour half of syrup mixture over each pan of popped corn. Bake for 30–40 minutes, stirring every 10 minutes. Remove from oven, cool completely; break apart. Store in tightly covered container. Serves 6–8.

Chocolate Chip Doozies

½ cup butter, room temperature
½ cup shortening
1 cup sugar
1 cup brown sugar, firmly packed
2 eggs
1 teaspoon vanilla extract
2¼ cups all-purpose flour
½ cup rolled oats
1 teaspoon baking soda

½ teaspoon salt
1 cup chocolate chips
1 cup coarsely chopped walnuts
1 cup miniature candy-coated chocolate pieces
½ cup raisins

Preheat oven to 375 degrees. Cream butter, shortening, and sugars; beat in eggs and vanilla. In small bowl, mix together flour, oats, baking soda, and salt. Add to creamed butter mixture. Stir in chocolate chips, walnuts, candy-coated chocolate pieces, and raisins. Drop by heaping ⅛ cup-fuls (a 2-tablespoon scoop) onto ungreased cookie sheets. Bake for 10–12 minutes. Cool several minutes on cookie sheets before removing to a cooling rack. MAKES 3 DOZEN LARGE COOKIES.

Carol Lanspeak herself waited on him. [Qwilleran] She and her husband were an admirable pair: good business heads, civic leaders, and major talents in the Pickax Theatre Club. If they had not come home to Pickax to run the family business, Qwilleran believed, Larry and Carol could have been another Cronyn and Tandy, or Lunt and Fontanne. (**Tailed a Thief**)

Cuttlebrink Reunion

CUTTLEBRINK SUMMER SOLSTICE REUNION SUPPER

We're *longing* to see you on the *longest* day of the year to share some "*long*" food with the *long*, tall people we've known the *longest*. Bring your *long* Italian foods . . . *long* pastas, *long* breads, *long* vegetables, and *long* desserts. If you can't think *long*, then just think Italian!

Place: Wildcat Pavilion

Date: June 21

Time: 5:00 P.M.

As they neared the county line, Qwilleran began to notice the name Cuttlebrink on rural mailboxes and then suddenly a roadside sign: WELCOME TO WILDCAT, POP. 95. A few hundred feet beyond, another sign suggested that the Cuttlebrinks had a sense of humor: YOU JUST PASSED WILDCAT. (**Knew a Cardinal**)

"Is Cuttlebrink Derek's real name?" [asked Clarissa]
"Absolutely! There's a town called Wildcat that's full of Cuttlebrinks." [said Qwilleran]
"Really? Where did it get its name?"
Railroad trains go wildcatting through small towns."
"Oh! What does that mean?"
"Going too fast in a controlled-speed zone."
"Oh!" (**Dropped a Bombshell**)

"What do you know about the famous wreck at Wildcat, Ozzie?" [asked Qwilleran]
"It weren't called Wildcat in them days. It were South Fork. Trains from up north slowed down to twenty at South Fork afore goin' down a steep grade to a mighty bad curve and a wood trestle bridge. The rails, they be a hun'erd feet over the water. One day a train come roarin' through South Fork, full steam, whistle screechin'. It were a wildcat—a runaway train—headed for the gorge. At the bottom—crash!—bang! Then hissing steam. Then dead quiet." (**Blew the Whistle**)

Beverages and Breads

Apricot Refresher

2 46-ounce bottles apricot nectar
4 cups pineapple juice
1 3-ounce can frozen orange juice concentrate, thawed
ice

Mix all ingredients except ice. Chill and serve over ice. MAKES APPROXIMATELY 1 GALLON.

Midnight Delight Iced Coffee

8 cups strong brewed coffee, chilled
3 cups half-and-half
⅓ cup sugar
2 teaspoons almond extract
crushed ice

Mix coffee, half-and-half, sugar, and almond extract together in large pitcher. Place crushed ice in glasses. Pour coffee over ice. SERVES 8.

Long Italian Breadsticks

⅓ cup butter
2½ cups all-purpose flour
1 tablespoon sugar
1 tablespoon baking powder
1 teaspoon salt
1 cup milk
Italian seasoning
garlic powder

Preheat oven to 425 degrees. Melt butter in oven in 9×13-inch pan. Remove pan from oven and set aside. Mix flour, sugar, baking powder, salt, and milk. Stir until dough holds together. Place on floured surface; turn over to coat both sides. Knead 10–12 times. Roll out to 8×12-inch rectangle. Cut dough into 12 1×8-inch strips. Place strips in buttered pan turning over to coat both sides with butter. Place in single row in pan. Sprinkle with Italian seasoning and garlic powder to taste. Bake 15–18 minutes. MAKES 12 STICKS.

Garlic Bread

1 large head garlic
olive oil
1 long *loaf Italian bread, sliced horizontally*
⅓ cup butter, room temperature

Preheat oven to 350 degrees. With sharp knife, cut top of garlic head off. Drizzle with oil. Place garlic in small pan or dish and cover with foil. Bake 45 minutes or until cloves are golden and tender. Squeeze garlic out of skins and spread on bottom half of the bread. Spread the top half of bread with butter. Put halves back together. Cover with foil. Bake 15 minutes. SERVES 6.

"This county [Moose] is full of curious names: Cuttlebrink, Dingleberry, Fitzbottom—almost Elizabethan. I used to have a Falstaff in one of my classes, and a Scroop. Straight out of Shakespeare, eh?" (**Knew Shakespeare**)

Salads and Sides

Derek's World's *Longest* Antipasto Tray

1 10-foot white vinyl rain gutter, cut down to 6 feet 8 inches, if desired

2 end caps for gutter (1 right and 1 left)

2 10-pound bags ice

9 feet heavy-duty aluminum foil

4 bunches leaf lettuce

1 canteloupe, sliced

1 pound each deli-sliced proscuitto, pepperoni, salami, and roast beef

1 pound each cubed mozzarella, Cheddar, and provolone cheeses

2 8-ounce jars olives

3 bell peppers (1 each red, green, and yellow) seeded, thinly sliced

1 pint cherry tomatoes

1 bunch carrots, peeled and julienned

1 red onion, sliced

12 red-skinned new potatoes, boiled and quartered

1 pound green beans, parboiled

1 bunch fresh parsley, chopped

Purchase a section of white vinyl rain gutter from a building supply or hardware store. (Gutters are usually sold in 10-foot sections but can be cut into a section that is 6 feet 8 inches long to match Derek Cuttlebrink's height.) Purchase right and left end caps for gutter. If desired, several small holes can be drilled low on each end cap to drain water from melting ice. Wash gutter with hot soapy water and dry. Assemble antipasto tray on location by spreading ice in gutter, covering ice with the 9-foot piece of foil. Be careful not to punch a hole in the foil to keep melted ice from coming into contact with food. Place leaf lettuce on foil. Wrap melon slices with proscuitto. Attractively arrange meats, cheeses, and vegetables on lettuce in gutter. Pour Dressing over vegetables. Sprinkle with chopped fresh parsley as desired. SERVES 25–30.

Dressing
¾ cup olive oil
½ cup red wine vinegar
2 tablespoons fresh lemon juice
3 tablespoons sugar
2 cloves garlic, minced
1 teaspoon oregano
½ teaspoon salt
¼ teaspoon pepper
fresh parsley

Whisk oil, vinegar, lemon juice, and sugar together until sugar dissolves. Stir in garlic, oregano, salt, pepper, and parsley. Pour over vegetables in antipasto tray.

"What's new in the restaurant business?" Qwilleran asked Hixie.
"Not much. We've just hired a busboy named Derek Cuttlebrink . . ." (Knew Shakespeare)

Summer Peach Salad

1½ cups finely chopped pecans
1¾ cups all-purpose flour
½ cup butter, melted
2 3-ounce packages peach gelatin
3 cups boiling water
3 cups diced peaches, canned or frozen
½ pint whipping cream
½ cup sugar
½ teaspoon almond extract
1 8-ounce package cream cheese, softened

Preheat oven to 350 degrees. Combine pecans, flour, and butter. Pat into bottom of 9×13-inch pan. Bake 15 minutes. Cool completely. Mix gelatin with water and stir until gelatin is dissolved. Cool slightly; add peaches and chill until slightly thickened. Whip cream until soft peaks form. Add sugar and almond extract. Beat in cream cheese. Mixture may be slightly lumpy. Spread cream cheese mixture over cooled crust. Gently spoon gelatin mixture over top. Chill until set. SERVES 12.

Lemon-Cherry Salad

---

1 8-ounce can crushed pineapple, undrained
⅓ cup sugar
1 cup water
1 3-ounce package lemon gelatin
1 3-ounce package cream cheese, softened
½ cup maraschino cherries, drained, quartered
½ cup chopped pecans

Heat pineapple, sugar, and water until boiling; add gelatin. Stir until gelatin dissolves. Cool slightly. Beat in cream cheese. Chill until partially set. Fold in cherries and pecans; chill until completely set. SERVES 6.

"We're used to chaos in community theatre, Qwill, but it always works out by opening night. [said Fran] Dwight did the casting and blocking before he left, and I worked with the supporting cast while you were away—the witches, the bleeding captain, the porter, and so forth. Derek Cuttlebrink is doing the porter in act two, scene three. Knock, knock, knock! Who's there? He'll provide our comic relief." (**Wasn't There**)

Pizza Macaroni Salad with *Long* Cheese

8 ounces seashell macaroni
8 1-ounce sticks string mozzarella cheese
2 medium tomatoes, cubed
¼ cup chopped onion
½ green pepper, diced
1 pound sliced pepperoni
½ cup vegetable oil
⅓ cup freshly grated Parmesan cheese
1 teaspoon dried oregano
½ teaspoon garlic powder
½ teaspoon salt
⅛ teaspoon pepper

Cook macaroni according to package directions; cool, drain. Separate each cheese stick into several long strings. Combine macaroni, mozzarella cheese strings, tomatoes, onion, green pepper, and pepperoni. Mix oil, Parmesan cheese, oregano, garlic powder, salt, and pepper. Stir into macaroni mixture. Chill for several hours. SERVES 8.

She [Polly] said, "I hear that Derek Cuttlebrink is playing the porter, and Dwight has him telescoping his six-feet-eight into a five-foot S-curve that will probably steal the show."

"I know Derek," said Trilby, swooping in with the entrees. "He's a sous-chef at the Old Mill."

"Very sous," Qwilleran muttered under his breath. (**Wasn't There**)

Long Green Beans in Bundles

1½ pounds fresh green beans
2 bunches green onions
½ cup olive oil
2 tablespoons cider vinegar
2 tablespoons capers
¼ teaspoon garlic powder
1 teaspoon dried basil
¼ teaspoon salt

𝒲𝒶𝓈𝒽 beans and remove ends. Do not break into pieces. Cut green stems from onions. Steam beans and green stems of onions until beans are tender-crisp. Place beans in bundles of 7–8 and tie with green onion stems. Finely chop remaining white sections of onions to make 2 tablespoons. Mix oil, vinegar, capers, and spices with onions and pour over bean bundles. Chill. MAKES APPROXIMATELY 24 BUNDLES.

Enter: a Visitor from outer space, almost seven feet tall. The audience howled as they recognized their favorite actor. He wore a Civil War uniform and sideburns and explained to the earthlings that he had miscalculated and landed in the wrong century. It was a challenging role for Derek, who was in almost every scene of the play. (**Saw Stars**)

Spaghetti Squash

1 small spaghetti squash (approximately 4–5 cups cooked squash)
1 clove garlic, finely chopped
1½ tablespoons butter
1 teaspoon dried basil
½ cup diced sun-dried tomatoes in oil, drained
salt and pepper to taste
¼ cup fresh, shredded, Parmesan cheese

Preheat oven to 350 degrees. Grease a casserole dish and set aside. Pierce whole squash in several places. Bake 45 minutes. Turn squash over and bake until squash yields to pressure, about 15 minutes. Let cool slightly. Cut in half and remove seeds. Scoop out *long* squash strands; place in bowl. In a small skillet, sauté garlic in butter; add basil. Pour butter mixture over squash; add tomatoes, salt, and pepper. Stir gently to mix. Place in prepared casserole dish, sprinkle with Parmesan cheese and bake for 10 minutes or until heated through. SERVES 4.

There was a moment's comic relief when Derek Cuttlebrink telescoped his youth and height into the arthritic shape of an ancient porter. "Knock, knock, knock! Who's there?" At intermission it was the French fry chef from the Old Stone Mill who was the topic of conversation in the lobby. (**Wasn't There**)

Long Carrot Casserole

2 pounds carrots
⅔ cup milk
⅔ cup brown sugar, firmly packed
8 tablespoons butter softened + 2 tablespoons butter, melted
½ cup + ¼ cup cracker crumbs
½ cup chopped green pepper
½ cup chopped onion
¼ teaspoon pepper

Preheat oven to 350 degrees. Lightly grease a 3-quart casserole dish. Slice, boil, and mash all but 2 carrots. Boil the 2 reserved long carrots whole and then cut lengthwise into 4 quarters. Set aside. Mix the mashed carrots, milk, sugar, and 8 tablespoons butter thoroughly. Fold in ½ cup cracker crumbs, green pepper, onion, and pepper. Pour into prepared casserole dish. Mix ¼ cup cracker crumbs and 2 tablespoons melted butter. Sprinkle on casserole. Use remaining long carrots to make a sunburst design decoration on top of crackers. Bake 35 minutes. SERVES 8–12.

The audience waited expectantly for another extraordinary dog, when who should amble on stage but the six-foot-eight Derek Cuttlebrink with his guitar. The audience screamed and applauded. (**Smelled a Rat**)

Artichoke Spread

2 12-ounce jars marinated artichoke hearts
1 cup mayonnaise
1 cup fresh grated Parmesan cheese
¼ teaspoon garlic powder
dash cayenne pepper
⅔ cup dry bread crumbs
4 teaspoons butter, melted
crackers or toast points

Preheat oven to 375 degrees. Drain, rinse, and coarsely chop artichokes. Mix together mayonnaise, Parmesan cheese, garlic, and pepper; add artichokes. Spread mixture in an ungreased pie plate. Mix together bread crumbs and butter. Sprinkle over artichoke mixture in pan. Bake 25–30 minutes. Serve with crackers or toast points. SERVES 8.

After Qwilleran and Polly were greeted and seated at their usual table, a six-foot-eight busboy, who towered above customers and staff alike, shuffled up to the table with a water pitcher and basket of garlic toast. His name was Derek Cuttlebrink.

"Hi, Mr. Q," he said in friendly fashion. "I thought you were going away for the summer."

"I came back," Qwilleran explained succinctly. (**Wasn't There**)

Bread-and-Butter Pickles

1¼ cup sugar
½ teaspoon turmeric
1 cup cider vinegar
1½ teaspoons salt
½ teaspoon celery seed
2 cloves garlic, slivered
4 cups thinly sliced pickling cucumbers
1 cup sliced onion

Bring sugar, turmeric, vinegar, salt, celery seed, and garlic to a boil. Place cucumbers and onions in large bowl. Pour boiling mixture over cucumbers and onions. Let stand for 1 hour. Place in jar or serving dish. MAKES APPROXIMATELY 1 QUART.

Meats

Spaghetti and Meatballs

Sauce

3 15-ounce cans tomato sauce
2 cloves garlic, minced
½ cup chopped onion
1 teaspoon sugar
1 teaspoon dried basil
1 bay leaf
½ teaspoon dried oregano
½ teaspoon marjoram
¼ teaspoon thyme
¼ teaspoon sage

In a saucepan, stir together tomato sauce, garlic, onion, sugar, and herbs. Simmer over low heat for 30 minutes, stirring periodically.

Meatballs

2 pounds lean ground beef
2 eggs
¼ cup minced onion
¼ cup bread crumbs
oil

Mix beef, eggs, onion, and bread crumbs. Shape into 1½-inch balls. Brown in oil. Add meatballs to sauce and simmer for 30 minutes. Serve over spaghetti. SERVES 6.

. . . *"I loved that young man who's so tall. Derek Cuttlebrink was the name in the program."* [said Celia]

Qwilleran assured her that there was a whole village full of Cuttlebrinks. "They're all characters!" he said. (**Blew the Whistle**)

Cheese Manicotti

1 8-ounce box manicotti (14 shells)
2 teaspoons dried basil
2 cloves garlic, minced
3 8-ounce cans tomato sauce
1 14½-ounce can diced tomatoes in sauce
3 cups ricotta cheese
2 cups + ½ cup mozzarella cheese
½ cup fresh grated Parmesan cheese
2 teaspoons dried parsley
2 eggs

Preheat oven to 350 degrees. Boil manicotti shells according to package directions. To make sauce, add basil and garlic to tomato sauce. Simmer over low heat while shells are boiling and during the preparation of filling. To make filling, mix together ricotta cheese, 2 cups mozzarella cheese, Parmesan cheese, parsley, and eggs. Stuff shells with filling. Place half the sauce in a 9x13-inch baking dish. Arrange shells in rows over sauce. Pour remaining sauce over shells, sprinkle remaining ½ cup mozzarella over top. Cover and bake for 50–60 minutes. SERVES 6–8.

*The audience exploded with cheers and laughter, and even Amanda managed a faint smile. Qwilleran said, "If elected, she should appoint Derek as court jester." (**Smelled a Rat**)*

Meat Lasagna

8 ounces lasagna noodles (9 noodles)
1 pound lean ground beef
⅛ cup dry bread crumbs
1 egg + 2 eggs
2 small cloves garlic, minced
2 15-ounce cans tomato sauce
2 teaspoons dried basil
½ teaspoon oregano
1 15-ounce container ricotta cheese
⅔ cup fresh, shredded Parmesan cheese
2 teaspoons dried parsley
2¼ cups mozzarella cheese

Preheat oven to 350 degrees. Lightly grease a 9×13-inch baking dish. Cook lasagna noodles in boiling water until tender. Mix beef, bread crumbs, and 1 egg. Cook meat mixture in a skillet with garlic, stirring to break the mixture into small pieces as it cooks. Drain excess fat. Stir in tomato sauce, basil, and oregano. Simmer over low heat for 20 minutes. In a separate bowl, mix ricotta cheese, Parmesan cheese, parsley, and 2 eggs. Place 3 cooked lasagna noodles in prepared baking dish. Top with ⅓ of the meat sauce, ½ of the ricotta cheese mixture, and ¾ cup mozzarella cheese. Place 3 additional noodles in pan. Repeat layer as before. Top mixture with remaining 3 noodles. Spoon remaining meat sauce and mozzarella cheese on top. Cover and bake 30–40 minutes. Remove from oven and allow lasagna to sit for at least 10 minutes before serving. Cut and serve in traditional square pieces or cut in *long* rectangular pieces. SERVES 8–10.

Qwilleran had known Derek since his days as a busboy, and always he treated CEOs and visiting bishops with the same offhand bonhomie that captivated the young girls who adored him. (**Saw Stars**)

Long Italian Sandwich

1 18-inch unsliced loaf of Italian bread
4 ounces (each) sliced deli ham, capacola, Genoa salami
2 ounces (each) provolone cheese, Italian fontina cheese
sliced tomato
thinly sliced onion
chopped bell pepper
chopped banana peppers
pitted olives
shredded lettuce
mayonnaise
brown mustard

Slice loaf horizontally and remove some of the bread from inside each crust; discard or save for future use. Arrange meats and cheeses on the bottom half of the bread. Top with tomato, onion, peppers, olives, and lettuce. Sprinkle with Dressing. Spread mayonnaise and mustard on top half of the bread. Slice into individual portions. SERVES 4 AS MEAL OR 8–10 AS APPETIZER.

Dressing
2 tablespoons red wine vinegar
1 tablespoon olive oil
½ teaspoon oregano
¼ teaspoon basil

¼ teaspoon thyme
salt and pepper to taste

Whisk all ingredients together. Allow to stand for at least 30 minutes for best flavor.

Italian Chicken

4 chicken breasts
½ cup all-purpose flour
1 teaspoon dried oregano leaves
1 teaspoon dried tarragon leaves
¼ teaspoon salt
⅛ teaspoon pepper
3 tablespoons butter
1 tablespoon oil
½ cup water
1 teaspoon fresh lemon juice

Preheat oven to 350 degrees. Mix flour, oregano, tarragon, salt, and pepper. Rinse chicken breasts; dredge in flour mixture. Heat butter and oil in skillet. Brown chicken in skillet and place in baking dish. Deglaze the skillet with the water. Add lemon juice to water and pour over chicken. Cover and bake 20 minutes. Remove cover and bake an additional 20 minutes. SERVES 4.

As soon as the two news staffers were seated in their favorite alcove, an exuberant and extremely tall waitperson bounced up to their table. "Hi, you guys," he [Derek] hailed them with the flip disrespect he reserved for VIP's. "I've been offered a new job."

"Here?" Qwilleran asked. "If they want to make you head chef, I'm taking my business elsewhere." (**Sang for the Birds**)

Desserts

Chocolate-Almond Biscotti

¾ cup sugar
3 tablespoons butter, softened
2 eggs
½ teaspoon almond extract
1½ cups all-purpose flour
½ cup cocoa
1½ teaspoons baking powder
½ teaspoon baking soda
½ cup sliced almonds

Preheat oven to 350 degrees. Grease a 9×5-inch loaf pan. In mixing bowl, beat sugar and butter until light and fluffy. Add eggs, one at a time. Stir in almond extract. In separate bowl, mix together flour, cocoa, baking powder, and baking soda. Slowly add dry ingredients to butter mixture. Fold in almonds. Smooth batter in prepared pan. Bake for 25 minutes. Remove from oven and cool in pan for 5 minutes. Reduce oven temperature to 300 degrees. Remove cake from pan and cut into eight 9×½-inch *long* strips or cut in traditional 5×½-inch pieces. Place on an ungreased cookie sheet and bake for an additional 20 minutes. Serves 8.

Italian Cream Cake

½ *cup butter, room temperature*
1 cup shortening
2 cups sugar
5 eggs, separated
2 cups all-purpose flour
1 teaspoon baking soda
1 cup buttermilk
1 teaspoon vanilla extract
1 3½-ounce can coconut
1 cup chopped pecans

Preheat oven to 350 degrees. Generously grease and flour 3 9-inch cake pans. Cream butter, shortening, and sugar until fluffy. Add egg yolks, one at a time. Mix flour and baking soda. Stir into sugar mixture, alternating with buttermilk, beginning and ending with flour mixture. Add vanilla, coconut, and pecans. Beat egg whites until stiff and fold into batter. Pour into prepared cake pans. Bake 30–35 minutes. Remove from pans. Cool on wire rack. Frost when cool. SERVES 12.

Frosting
¾ cup butter, room temperature
1 8-ounce and 1 3-ounce package cream cheese
6 cups powdered sugar
1 teaspoon vanilla extract
24 pecan halves
1 3½-ounce can coconut

Cream butter and cream cheese together. Add powdered sugar and vanilla. Mix well. Add a little milk if frosting is too stiff. Frost top and sides of cake; garnish with pecans and coconut.

"Good! I want you [Derek] to listen to the scuttlebutt and report to me what you hear." [said Qwilleran] He knew that would come naturally for Derek. As a native of Moose County, he had been weaned on gossip . . . "You're a good actor, Derek. You can carry this off without blowing your cover, and you make friends easily; people will be glad to talk to you. If they know anything, they'll be only too glad to spill it in a safe ear." (**Came to Breakfast**)

Dottie's Spotties

½ cup shortening
4 1-ounce squares semisweet baking chocolate
2 cups sugar
2 teaspoons vanilla extract
4 eggs
2 cups all-purpose flour
2 teaspoons baking powder
⅛ teaspoon salt
½ cup chopped walnuts
½ cup powdered sugar

Preheat oven to 350 degrees. Generously grease a cookie sheet. Melt shortening and chocolate. Pour into mixing bowl. Stir in sugar and vanilla. Beat in eggs, one at a time. In a separate bowl, mix together flour, baking powder, and salt. Add to chocolate mixture. Stir in walnuts. Chill 1 hour. Form into small balls about 1¼ inches in diameter. Roll in powdered sugar. Place 2 inches apart on prepared cookie sheet. Bake 12 minutes. MAKES 6 DOZEN COOKIES.

Angie's Strawberry Mascarpone Pie

1 15-ounce package rolled pie crusts
sugar
1 pint whipping cream
½ cup powdered sugar
1 teaspoon vanilla extract
1 8-ounce container mascarpone cheese
1 pint fresh strawberries, sliced

Preheat oven to 450 degrees. Unroll pie crusts and place on two ungreased cookie sheets. Sprinkle with water and sugar. Cut pie crusts into 8 wedges and slide wedges apart slightly. Bake 10 minutes or until golden brown. Remove from oven and allow to cool. Beat whipping cream until stiff peaks form. Add powdered sugar and vanilla. Remove half of whipping cream and set aside. Add mascarpone cheese to remaining whipping cream; beat until blended. To assemble dessert; place one wedge of pie crust on platter; top with dollop of mascarpone mixture. Add several strawberry slices. Top with another wedge of pie crust. Add plain whipping cream and more strawberries on top. Assemble all 8 wedges and place back into round on serving platter. Sprinkle with cinnamon. SERVES 8.

As Derek Cuttlebrink sauntered over with water pitcher and bread basket, the superintendent [Lyle Compton] said with his usual cynical scowl, "Here comes our most distinguished alumnus."

"Hi, Mr. Compton," said the gregarious busboy. "Did you see me in the play?"

"I certainly did, Derek, and you were head and shoulders above all the others."

"Gee." (**Knew a Cardinal**)

Chocolate Yardstick

2 eggs, separated
½ cup sugar
¾ cup finely chopped hazelnuts
2 ounces semisweet baking chocolate, grated
1 sheet frozen puff pastry, thawed

Preheat oven to 400 degrees. Mix together egg yolks, sugar, nuts, and chocolate. With mixer, beat egg whites until stiff. Fold into chocolate mixture. Unfold pastry and place on floured surface. Use rolling pin to roll pastry into 12×18-inch rectangle. Cut pastry lengthwise into 2 6×18-inch pastry sheets. Place one sheet of dough diagonally across an ungreased cookie sheet. Place half the filling in a strip in the middle of the dough. Fold up sides of dough and use water to seal the pastry on top of the filling. Sprinkle with water and additional sugar. Repeat procedure with remaining dough and filling. It is very important to seal the top and ends of dough securely so filling does not cook out during baking. Bake for 20–25 minutes. SERVES 12.

Lemon Gelato

8 cups milk
1 teaspoon lemon zest
12 egg yolks
3 cups sugar
1 cup fresh lemon juice

In large saucepan, scald milk (150 degrees). Add lemon zest. Remove milk from heat. Mix egg yolks and sugar thoroughly. Slowly stir 2 cups scalded milk into egg mixture, stirring constantly. Return egg mixture to remaining milk in pan. Return to heat and cook until slightly thickened;

stirring constantly. Do not boil. Chill. Add lemon juice. Place mixture in ice-cream maker and follow manufacturer's directions for freezing ice cream. SERVES 8–10.

Derek Cuttlebrink had the height (six feet eight) and the outgoing nature that gave him carte blanche around town, and he assumed that everyone was interested in his personal life. His customers enjoyed his breezy style; young women adored him; audiences at the theater club's productions were wild about Derek's performances. Now, to his credit, he had enrolled in the restaurant management program at the Moose County Community College. At last he was being viewed by serious observers as a "comer" and not just an engaging clown. (**Sang for the Birds**)

There were those who thought the young man [Derek] scatter-brained, but Qwilleran was confident that he had promise. Inside that lanky, goofy kid there was a short, serious young man trying to find himself. (**Came to Breakfast**)

Cat Reunion

"Have you had any more crazy dreams?" she [Polly] asked.

"Yes, I dreamed that Koko and Yum Yum gave a party for Brutus and Catta. And they invited Toulouse and Jet Stream because a successful party always has more male guests than female guests." [said Qwilleran]

Between her laughter she said, "I don't know anyone who dreams as fancifully and creatively as you do!" (**Smelled a Rat**)

❖

HONORED GUEST LIST

Jet Stream in care of Wetherby Goode

Brutus and Catta in care of Polly Duncan

Sarah Bernhardt, Louisa May Alcott, Carrie Nation, Charlotte Brontë, and Flora Macdonald in care of Maggie Sprenkle

Winston Churchill in care of Bethunes

Toulouse in care of Rikers

Nicodemus in care of Nutcracker Inn

Wrigley in care of Celia Robinson O'Dell

Dundee in care of the Pirate's Chest

Katie and Mac in care of Pickax Library

Quincy in care of Mayor Amanda Goodwinter

In the still of the night

When no one is looking

Come to our house

And enjoy our cooking.

Come in the back door

To join our party.

The fun begins at twelve,

So don't be tardy.

This secret family bond

That we all share

Is what we'll celebrate

With our feline flair.

RSVP Koko and Yum Yum in care of Qwilleran's Apple Barn

Unlocking his door and reaching for the light switch, Qwilleran discovered that the foyer and other rooms were already lighted, although he distinctly remembered leaving the apartment in darkness, except for the bathroom.

"Who's here?" he demanded. Koko and Yum Yum came running. They showed no symptoms of terror, no indication that an intruder had threatened them. They were simply aware that Qwilleran was carrying a packet of veal, scallops, and squid. (**Lived High**)

Scallops in Gruyere Sauce

2 cups water
1 tablespoon + 1 tablespoon lemon juice
½ teaspoon salt
2 pounds scallops, washed, drained
½ cup canned mushrooms, drained
¼ cup chopped onions
4 tablespoons + 2 tablespoons butter
⅓ cup all-purpose flour
1½ cups half-and-half
1 cup grated Gruyere cheese
½ cup white wine or water
1 tablespoon chopped fresh parsley
½ cup dry, fine bread crumbs

Bring water, 1 tablespoon lemon juice, and salt to a boil. Add scallops and simmer 7 minutes or until tender; drain. Saute mushrooms and onions in 4 tablespoons butter until tender. Remove from heat and stir in flour. Return to heat and pour in half-and-half, stirring constantly until thickened. Add cheese and stir until melted. Stir in wine or water, 1 tablespoon lemon juice, and parsley. Add scallops. Pour into 1½-quart casserole. Melt 2 tablespoons butter; mix with bread crumbs; sprinkle on scallop mixture. Broil 2–3 minutes or until golden brown. SERVES 12 CATS OR 8 HUMANS.

He [Qwilleran] opened a can of minced clams for the Siamese and said, "Okay, you guys. Try to stay out of trouble while I'm gone. I'm going to visit your cousin Bootsie." (**Said Cheese**)

. . . they gobbled it with gusto, spitting out the onion fastidiously. (**Tailed a Thief**)

Clams Au Gratin

1 cup small shell macaroni
1 cup soft bread crumbs
1 cup shredded Cheddar cheese
1 tablespoon chopped onion
½ cup melted butter
1 teaspoon salt
⅛ teaspoon pepper
2 6½-ounce cans minced clams, drained, liquid reserved
1½ cups clam liquid and milk
2 eggs, beaten

Preheat oven to 350 degrees. Prepare macaroni according to package directions, drain. Mix bread crumbs, cheese, onion, butter, salt, pepper, clams, and liquid. Blend in eggs and macaroni. Pour in well-greased 1½-quart casserole. Bake 40–45 minutes or until cooked in center. SERVES 8 CATS OR 6–8 HUMANS.

As the manager totaled the array of salmon, crab, lobster, chicken, and shrimp he asked [Qwilleran] politely, "Are you with a group?" (**Moved a Mountain**)

Feeding two fussy felines was another more immediate, more exasperating problem. They had been on a seafood binge, and he had stocked up on canned clams, tuna, crabmeat, and cocktail shrimp. (**Said Cheese**)

Seafood Salad

1 6-ounce can chunk white albacore tuna, drained
2 4-ounce cans deveined medium shrimp, drained
1 6-ounce can fancy white crab meat, drained
1 cup finely chopped celery
3 hard-boiled eggs, chopped
2 tablespoons capers
½ cup mayonnaise or to taste
salt and pepper to taste
lettuce

Mix tuna, shrimp, and crab meat. Add celery, eggs, and capers. Gently fold in mayonnaise. Add salt and pepper. Chill. Serve on lettuce. (Koko and Yum Yum will serve on catnip.) SERVES 6 CATS OR 4 HUMANS.

On this particular morning, the Siamese were treated to a serving of choice red salmon—two servings, his and hers. There followed an interval for catly ablutions, a ritual that only they could understand. Next they were groomed with their favorite brush—a silver-backed antique that had belonged to the late Iris Cobb. (**Talked Turkey**)

"Do your spoiled brats eat codfish?" Lois inquired as she banged the keys on the old-fashioned machine. "Tomorrow's special—fish 'n' chips."

"Thank you. I'll consult them." [said Qwilleran] He knew very well that Koko and Yum Yum turned up their well-bred noses at anything less than top-grade red sockeye salmon. (**Sang for the Birds**)

Baked Salmon

1½–2 pounds salmon
dried dill weed
3 large cloves garlic, minced
1 small onion, finely chopped
salt
pepper
2 lemons, sliced

Preheat oven to 425 degrees. Cut salmon into serving-sized pieces; place all pieces on 1 large piece of foil. Sprinkle liberally with dill weed, garlic, and onion. Add salt and pepper to taste. Top with lemon slices. Wrap in foil. Bake 20–25 minutes or until fish flakes easily with a fork (or a paw). SERVES 8 CATS OR 6–8 HUMANS.

"We'll try it once more . . . Would you like some turkey?" [asked Qwilleran]

Koko's eye's popped open, and Yum Yum raised her head abruptly. With one accord the two of them jumped to the floor, yipping and squealing as they raced to the refrigerator, where Quilleran found them arranged in identical poses, like twins, as they stared up at the door handle. (**Sniffed Glue**)

Koko was not present to cast his vote, but Yum Yum was rubbing against Qwilleran's ankles in anticipation and curling her tail lovingly around his leg, and he knew she preferred turkey. (**Underground**)

Turkey Scallopini

1 pound boneless turkey cutlets
1 tablespoon + ¼ cup vegetable oil
2 tablespoons brown sugar, firmly packed
2 tablespoons spicy brown mustard
2 tablespoons lemon juice
1 clove garlic, minced
salt and pepper to taste

Fry turkey in 1 tablespoon oil for approximately 2 minutes on each side. Whisk rest of ingredients together and pour over turkey. Simmer 10 minutes. SERVES 8 CATS OR 4 HUMANS.

Qwilleran put a plate of canned red salmon on the floor in the laundry room and called the cats. Yum Yum reported immediately but there was no response from Koko. "Drat him!" He's gone up to the attic again," Qwilleran muttered. (**Played Post Office**)

Salmon Loaf

2 6-ounce cans salmon
1½ cups herb-seasoned stuffing mix
2 tablespoons finely chopped onions
½ cup finely chopped celery
2 eggs
1 cup sour cream
½ cup half-and-half
salt and pepper to taste

Preheat oven to 350 degrees. Grease a 9×5-inch loaf pan. Mix all ingredients together. Place in prepared loaf pan. Bake 55–60 minutes or until center of loaf is firm. SERVES 6–8 CATS OR 4–6 HUMANS.

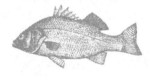

Just for Fun

"We have a colony of fruit flies that came with the apple barn, and they come out of hibernation at this time of year. Koko catches them on the wing and munches them as hors d'oeuvres." [said Qwilleran] (**Wasn't There**)

Chocolate-Covered "Fruit Flies"

¼ cup creamy peanut butter
½ cup powdered sugar
60 almond slices
3 2-ounce squares chocolate-flavored bark coating or any dipping chocolate

Mix peanut butter and powdered sugar until a smooth paste forms. Shape into approximately 30 half-teaspoonful-sized "fruit fly" bodies. Insert 1 almond "wing" on each side of the "body." Chill "flies" while melting chocolate. Hold each fly on a fork while spooning melted chocolate over body and wings. Place on wax paper; refrigerate until chocolate sets. MAKES ABOUT 30.

Qwilleran reached down and retrieved a notebook—a school notebook with torn and ruffled pages. Koko immediately jumped out of his hiding place, yowling and demanding his treasure. Some of the pages had obviously been nibbled by mice. (**Played Post Office**)

Devilish "Mice"

6 eggs
¼ cup mayonnaise
1 tablespoon sweet pickle relish, drained
salt to taste
pepper to taste
36 tiny pimiento pieces
48 1-inch-long pieces uncooked spaghetti
12 1-inch-long pieces red licorice strings

𝒫lace eggs in saucepan with enough cold water to cover. Bring to a boil. Reduce heat and let simmer 15 minutes. Cool, and remove shells. Cut in half lengthwise. Remove yolks and mix with mayonnaise and relish. Add salt and pepper to taste. Put yolk mixture back into whites. Arrange on serving plate, yolk side down. With the tip of a small knife, cut 3 tiny holes in the narrow end of the white part of the egg, representing eyes and nose of each "mouse." Insert pimiento pieces into the holes. Place 2 pieces of spaghetti on each side of the nose as whiskers. Insert 1 piece of licorice in the other end for a tail. Repeat for other 11 "mice." (Remove "whiskers" before eating.) MAKES 12 MICE.

Both cats [Koko and Yum Yum] had the shaded fawn bodies and brown points of pedigreed seal-point Siamese: brown masks accentuating the blueness of their eyes; alert brown ears worn like royal crowns; brown legs elegantly long and slender; brown tails that lashed and curled and waved to express emotions and opinions. But Koko had something more: a disconcerting degree of intelligence and an uncanny knack of knowing when something was . . . wrong! (**Knew Shakespeare**)

"Would you like a warm drink before you turn in? At the risk of sounding like your mother, I recommend cocoa." [said Qwilleran] (**Robbed a Bank**)

Koko's Cocoa

¾ cup cocoa
1½ cups sugar
¾ cup + 6 cups milk
brandy, mint, and/or orange extracts
1 can whipped cream

𝓜𝓲𝔁 cocoa, sugar, and ¾ cup milk until smooth in large saucepan. Slowly add remaining milk while stirring. Heat to desired temperature. Pour into 6 mugs. Before serving, add ⅛ teaspoon of desired extract flavor to each mug and top with whipped cream. SERVES 6.

"Treat!" he [Qwilleran] said in a stage whisper.
Two heads popped up!
"Yow!" came Koko's clamoring response.
"N-n-now!" shrieked Yum Yum. (**Saw Stars**)

Cat Chow

¼ cup butter
1 cup creamy peanut butter
12 ounces semisweet chocolate chips
8 cups rice cereal squares
5 cups round honey graham cereal
1 16-ounce box powdered sugar

𝓜𝓮𝓵𝓽 butter, peanut butter, and chocolate chips in a large saucepan over low heat. Remove from heat. Add cereal and mix gently until covered. Put powdered sugar in large plastic bag. Add cereal mixture and shake until evenly covered with powdered sugar. Place in shallow pan 3 hours to set chocolate. Store in airtight container. SERVES 10–12.

She [Lori Bamba] had long golden hair, which she braided and tied with ribbons, and these tempting appendages held a hypnotic fascination for the Siamese, who greeted her with enthusiastic prowling and ankle rubbing. (**Knew a Cardinal**)

"But it's true that cats respond to blue. Yellow and blue are the colors they see best, although they live in a world of fuzzy pastels." [said Dr. Constable] (**Went Bananas**)

Lori Bamba's Braids and Bows

1 12-ounce package white chocolate chips
24 pretzel rods
1 ounce yellow decorating sugar
4 sheets blue fruit leather snacks

𝓜𝓮𝓵𝓽 white chocolate morsels according to package directions. Spoon chocolate over pretzel rods, coating the rod with chocolate but leaving 2 inches bare at the end of the pretzel. Place on wax paper on a cookie sheet. Sprinkle with decorating sugar. Cut each sheet of the fruit leather into 6 2½-inch by 1½-inch pieces. Twist each piece of the fruit leather in the center to resemble a bow. Place the fruit leather "bow" about one inch above the end of the chocolate-coated end of the pretzel. Chill in the refrigerator to set the chocolate. MAKES 24 "BRAIDS."

At the water's edge seven crows strutted nonchalantly. Trout jumped out of the water for skee-ters, causing Koko to jerk his head excitedly this way and that. Then his body stiffened; Qwill-eran could feel the tension on his shoulder. Did the cat see an otter swimming, or a raccoon on the opposite shore? No, something was drifting down the creek. (**Went Up the Creek**)

Catch of the Day

¾ cup shortening
1 cup sugar
1 egg
¼ cup molasses
3 cups all-purpose flour
2 teaspoons ground ginger
½ teaspoon ground cinnamon
2 teaspoons baking soda
½ teaspoon salt
green, yellow, and blue decorating sugars
10 strings red licorice

Cream shortening and sugar until light and fluffy. Beat in egg and molasses. Mix flour, ginger, cinnamon, baking soda, and salt together in a separate bowl. Stir into sugar mixture to form dough. Wrap dough in plastic wrap and chill overnight in refrigerator. Preheat oven to 350 degrees. Roll dough out on floured surface to ¼-inch thickness. Use sharp knife to cut dough into 4×2½-inch fish shapes. Place cutouts on an ungreased cookie sheet. Use a drinking straw to cut small circle in head of the fish. Sprinkle heavily with all three decorating sugars to create iridescent "scales" of fish. Bake for 10 to 12 minutes. It may be necessary to repunch the hole in the head of the fish cookie immediately after baking. Remove cookies to cooling rack. When cooled, string 3 or 4 fish on each string of licorice to create the "catch of the day." MAKES 3 DOZEN FISH.

He [Qwilleran] lay down again. Then he became aware of intermittent flashes of light. He swung out of bed and hurried into the living room. A greenish light so powerful that it filtered through the louvered shutters was coloring the white walls, white sofas, and even Koko's pale fur a ghastly tint. The cat was on the arm of the sofa, his back humped, his tail bushed, his ears back, his eyes staring at the front window. (**Went Underground**)

Koko's Flying Saucers

24 fudge-striped graham cookies
12 large marshmallows
9 2-ounce blocks chocolate-flavored candy coating
miniature candy-coated chocolate pieces

𝒜rrange graham cookies on cookie sheet lined with wax paper. Cut marshmallows in half; place sticky side down on each of the graham cookies. Melt dipping chocolate according to package directions. Pick up each graham cookie with marshmallow individually and spoon chocolate over it, allowing excess chocolate to drip back into bowl. Place cookie back on wax paper. After all cookies have been covered, stick candy-coated chocolate pieces around top and/or edges of marshmallows to resemble lights on flying saucers. Chill in the refrigerator until chocolate is set. MAKES 24 "FLYING SAUCERS."

At that moment there were two soft thumps to be heard, and Yum Yum descended from her lofty perch. She walked slowly and sinuously past the kitchen table, each velvet paw touching the floor like a caress. (**Moved a Mountain**)

The female [Yum Yum] was developing an inordinate affection for the man. [Qwilleran] She was brazenly possessive of his lap. She gazed at him with adoring eyes, purred when he looked her way, and liked nothing better than to reach up and touch his moustache with a velvet paw. (**Knew Shakespeare**)

Yum Yum's Velvet Paws

1 cup butter, softened
1 cup + ¾ cup powdered sugar
1 teaspoon vanilla extract
2½ cups all-purpose flour
1 cup chopped hazelnuts
2 tablespoons cocoa

Preheat oven to 350 degrees. Grease a cookie sheet and set aside. Mix together butter and 1 cup powdered sugar until smooth. Blend in vanilla. Add flour and nuts; mix thoroughly. Shape into ovals about 2¼ inches long and ¾ inch wide using about 1 tablespoonful of dough. Place on prepared cookie sheet and bake for 20 minutes. Mix cocoa and ¾ cup powdered sugar. Cool cookies slightly; roll in powdered sugar mixture. Makes 3 dozen "velvet paws."

Qwilleran had always attributed the cat's [Koko] foresight to his sixty whiskers—sixty instead of the standard forty-eight; but, perhaps that crafty little animal had also been sitting in the bowl-shaped seat of the twistle-twig and thinking extraordinary thoughts. (**Dropped a Bombshell**)

Sitting in the kitchen observing the grooming ritual, Qwilleran asked himself, What does Koko have that other cats do not? The answer was: Sixty whiskers, eyebrows included, and counting both sides of his noble head. (**Robbed a Bank**)

Koko's Whiskers

1 sheet frozen puff pastry, thawed
½ cup butter, melted
½ cup sugar

𝒫reheat oven to 400 degrees. Line a cookie sheet with foil and grease foil. Unroll the puff pastry on work area. Cut pastry into ½×10-inch strips. Twist to make long twisted "whiskers." Place on cookie sheet; brush with butter and sprinkle with sugar. Press ends down to keep in place and remain twisted while baking. Bake 12–15 minutes or until golden brown. Makes 24 "whiskers."

She [Yum Yum] was on the seat of the sofa, thrusting first one paw and then the other behind a cushion. As the mumblings and fumblings became frantic, he went to her aid. As soon as he removed the seat cushion, she pounced on a half-crumpled piece of paper and carried it to the porch in her jaws, to be batted around for a few seconds and then forgotten. (**Came to Breakfast**)

Yum Yum was on her hind legs searching the wastebasket for crumpled paper, which had an irresistible attraction for her. (**Knew a Cardinal**)

Yum Yum's Crumpled Papers

1 cup fresh shredded Parmesan cheese

𝒫reheat oven to 375 degrees. Line a cookie sheet with foil and lightly grease. Place cheese by tablespoonfuls into circles about 3 inches in diameter. Place 2–3 inches apart. Bake 6–8 minutes. Remove from oven and lift foil from pan; place entire piece of foil with cheese circles on a cooling rack. Carefully crumple foil under the cheese circles to achieve a "crumpled paper" look in the cheese. Let cheese cool and remove carefully from foil. MAKES 10–12 "CRUMPLED PAPERS."

"But cats make wonderful models," said Vicki. "They never strike a pose that isn't photogenic."
Qwilleran huffed lightly into his moustache. "I dispute that. Every time I think I'm getting a good snapshot, my cats yawn or turn into pretzels, and nothing is less picturesque than a cat's gullet or his backside." (**Went Underground**)

Catzels (Cat Pretzels)

1-pound loaf frozen bread dough
1 egg, beaten with 1 teaspoon water
coarse salt
cinnamon
coarse sugar

Preheat oven to 375 degrees. Grease a cookie sheet and set aside. Thaw bread dough in microwave oven according to package directions. Slice dough in half and roll or squeeze each half into a rope approximately 32-inches long. To achieve a pretzel that resembles a cat, take one rope and shape it into an upside-down U on prepared cookie sheet. Holding on to the ends, twist the dough once about 8 inches from the ends and then tuck the ends under the upside-down U. The knot should be placed inside the U. Extend the ends of the dough out from under the original U end to appear as whiskers of a cat. Pinch both lower double-arches to form "cat ears." Repeat with the second rope of dough. Lightly brush both "catzels" with egg; sprinkle one with salt to create feisty Koko and sprinkle one with a mixture of cinnamon and sugar to create sweet Yum Yum. Bake for 15–18 minutes. SERVES 4.

Though not especially designed to be cat-friendly, that was what the barn proved to be . . . The ramp was made-to-order for a fifty-yard dash; before each meal, eight thundering paws spiraled to the top and down again. Odd-shaped windows admitted triangles and rhomboids of sunlight that tantalized the cats by moving throughout the day. (**Sang for the Birds**)

Barn Windows

½ cup butter
1 12-ounce package semisweet chocolate chips
½ cup chopped pecans
1 10½-ounce white miniature marshmallows

𝓜𝓮𝓵𝓽 butter and chocolate chips in a large pan. Remove from heat. Stir in pecans and then marshmallows. Place wax paper on a cookie sheet. Pour mixture onto wax paper in one 15-inch log or form 2 smaller logs, if desired. Wrap in wax paper and chill until hardened. Cut into slices to serve. Marshmallows form the triangle and rhomboid "windows" with chocolate "frames." Store unused portion in refrigerator. MAKES 30 ½-INCH SLICES.

When he [Qwilleran] returned to Cabin Five, he found that the Siamese had devised their own farewell: All the built-in drawers on nylon rollers were open—all twenty-three of them! Who could say that animals have no sense of humor? (**Went up the Creek**)

"The way to have a friend is to be a friend," said Qwilleran, *"and that goes double for cats."* (**Smelled a Rat**)

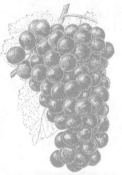

After-Dinner Catly Games and Contests

Pin the Leash on the Dog

Yarn Ball Unraveling Contest

Paper Bag Hide-and-Seek

High Jump

Broad Jump

Loudest Meow

Sharpest Claws

Catnip Ball Roll

Wastebasket Treasure Hunt

Choose from These Stimulating Lectures

Cheeses of the World
Birds: Friends or Foe?
Flying Saucer Lore
Alien Cats: Myth or Reality?
Famous Felines in History
Owner Training Made Easy

Metric Equivalents

VOLUME

Slightly less than ¼ teaspoon	1 ml
Slightly less than ½ teaspoon	2 ml
1 teaspoon	5 ml
1 tablespoon	15 ml
1 tablespoon plus 2 teaspoons	25 ml
⅛ cup	30 ml
¼ cup minus 2 teaspoons	50 ml
¼ cup	60 ml
⅓ cup	80 ml
½ cup	125 ml
⅔ cup	160 ml
¾ cup	180 ml
1 cup	250 ml
1 pint plus 2 tablespoons	500 ml
1 quart plus ¼ cup	1 liter

SOLIDS

1 ounce plus a large pinch	30 g
¼ pound	125 g
½ pound plus less than 1 ounce	250 g
1 pound plus 1⅔ ounces	500 g
1½ pounds plus about 2½ ounces	750 kg
2 pounds plus about 3½ ounces	1000 g (1 kg)
1 cup all-purpose flour (about 4 ounces)	about 112 g
1 cup granulated sugar (about 8 ounces)	about 224 g
8 tablespoons butter (4 ounces = 1 stick)	125 g

COOKING TEMPERATURES

Degrees Celsius		Degrees Fahrenheit	Gas Mark
150	Slow oven	300	2
158	Slow oven	325	3
177	Moderate oven	350	4
190	Moderately hot oven	375	5
204	Hot oven	400	6
214	Hot oven	425	7
232	Very hot oven	450	8
260	Very hot oven	500	9

Index

Rich Chocolate Cake, 112
Scottish Cottage Pudding, 80
Tartan Cake, 81
The Uglies, 158
Whiskey Cake, 160